TALES FROM STOOL 17 - FINDING PORT ST. JOE

THE NIGEL LOGAN ACTION SERIES #1

KIRK S. JOCKELL

THE FREE MULLET PRESS, LLC

Book Design by The Free Mullet Press, LLC

Cover Design by Cover2Book.com

Author Photo by Debbie Hooper Photography

PRINTED IN THE UNITED STATES OF AMERICA

DEDICATION

For Randy "RanDaddy" Everett

They say folks come down here to find themselves or hide;
I suppose I've done a little of both and managed to find some peace of mind.
--Brian Bowen, Indian Pass

Numbers

They're ubiquitous, numbers I mean. From their use in counting and calculations, to the less mathematical application of labeling things. Numbers are everywhere. Think about it. If you stopped reading right now and looked up, chances are you will find at least one number, probably more. You may need to turn your head to the right or the left, but they are there.

My name is Nigel Logan, a retired chief from the world's finest United States Navy. I spent the best part of twenty-three years as a QM, a quartermaster, a navigator. I make sure ships get from point A to point B. I've made a career of pouring over charts and stars and electronic technology to track my ships' whereabouts and movement.

Lord knows, I dealt with numbers every day: latitudes, longitudes, azimuths, compass headings, speed, time, distance, sight tables, and soundings. Those only scratch the surface.

In the Navy, we number everything. It's our favorite labeling system. From bow numbers to buildings, everything gets a number, even bar stools. Mine was stool seventeen. Let me explain.

There were twenty-three barstools at the enlisted club on the Little Creek Amphibious Base. Each stool had a number on the back, a brass plaque engraved with its number spelled across the center in cursive. Each morning, the barkeeps made sure they neatly placed all the stools in order: number one through twenty-five. Stools five and eleven were missing, perhaps retired after years of faithful service, or more probably, broken after the occasional fight.

I was a wet-behind-the-ears sailor with plenty of time left on my contract and no clue what the future held. I was fresh out of boot camp, Great Lakes, Illinois. Unlike most of the shipmates I graduated with, I was a late bloomer... sort of. I entered the service at twenty and enjoyed my 21st birthday while standing the mid-watch. So, the day I graduated, I was ready for a drink.

Stool seventeen's fifteenth position placed it right in front of the draft beer station. On most days after work, you could find there enjoying a libation or two. Liberty was a privilege I always did my best to make the most of. It was 1987. Pitchers of draft beer were a buck eighty, the perfect price for a budget-minded squid. Those were the days.

Over time I earned a stake, a homestead claim, to that spot at the bar. Stool seventeen was mine. The bartenders would keep it open for me, for a reasonable amount of time, anyway. *Hey sailor, you can't sit there yet. That's Logan's seat.*

The number seventeen became an inside joke on the ship amongst enlisted and officers alike. It didn't matter what the question was; the answer was always the same. What's going on tonight? *Seventeen.* Has anyone seen Logan? *Seventeen.* What cha think'n bout? *Seventeen.*

One morning our division was standing at quarters, the morning muster. Our Chief was giving us a quick inspection. When he got to me, he studied me with an eye of scrutiny. He could tell the previous night had been a little long in the making. He asked, "How are we feeling this morning, Logan?"

"Four-oh and improving, Chief." Four-Oh... a reference to the highest score one could get on a performance evaluation.

Chief laughed. "You look like shit. Are you going to be all right today?"

"Don't try to keep up, Chief. You'll be panting all day."

He liked that. "Logan, you're so full of crap it's running out your ears. Just how many beers did you have last night?"

Before I said anything, all my shipmates piped up in unison and shouted, "Seventeen, Chief!"

It hurt to smile.

My first ship was the USS Ponce, LPD-15. She, like my barstool, was berthed at Little Creek. I spent over four years aboard her. I was an undesignated seaman, meaning I had no other naval profession but chipping old paint and slapping on new. It serves as a great motivator to encourage initiative to improve one's naval career.

It would be the watches I spent on the bridge that exposed me to navigation. I was later authorized to strike for the Quartermaster rating. *Strike...* the term used to indicate one's on-the-job-training into a naval rating, a profession. By the time I left the ship, I was a second class petty officer, a QM2. I had a promising career, the respect of my shipmates, and glowing references from the chiefs and officers over me.

With new orders to Mayport, FL in hand, I departed the ship for the last time as ship's company. I was met at the ship's brow by the Officer of the Watch. I saluted, "Permission to go ashore, sir."

He saluted back, "Permission granted." We dropped our salutes together. Then he asked with a smile, "So Logan, where are you going to do your drinking now?"

"It doesn't really matter anymore, sir," I said with an even bigger smile. "Any stool in any port will always be number seventeen." I reached in my back pocket and produced the brass plaque from my old bar stool. "The bartenders gave it to me. They said it wouldn't be right for me to leave without it. I didn't argue."

I put the plaque back in my pocket and turned with a snap. I saluted the ensign flying at the stern and held it longer than I normally would have. Then I turned and headed down to the pier, stool seventeen in my back pocket.

Almost two decades later, you can find me on a slice of rural coastal paradise, Port St. Joe. It is on the Florida Panhandle and serves as the "big city" for Cape San Blas, Indian Pass, and all of Gulf County. It is a small town, but it's upscale too. We even have traffic lights, two of them. And, to top things off, we have a Piggly Wiggly. Who could ask for more? The one thing we are not is your typical gulf coast tourist trap.

My arrival wasn't totally accidental. My retirement from the Navy came suddenly and prematurely. I never planned to leave service as soon as I did, but the one thing my new freedom instilled was a need to get away.

I was stationed on a ship that made berth in Norfolk, Virginia. I wasn't running away, but given the circumstances, it was best that I left. If others wanted to find me, it wouldn't be impossible, but I wouldn't make it easy for them either.

My home away from the ship is *MisChief*, a 1966 Pearson Vanguard, a 32-foot blue water sailboat of classic design. With a moon that was new and the cloak of darkness on my side, I fired up the diesel, untied my dock lines, and eased out of the marina with no running lights. With her dark blue hull, she was almost invisible in the night. If someone was still watching, they would have needed to pay very close attention. Aside from some surface lighting from shore, it was pitch black. But with the aid of my night vision binoculars, I could see well enough.

The wind blew a steady 12 to 15 knots, perfect conditions but on the nose all the way to the Chesapeake Bay Bridge Tunnel. Under sail, it was a beat the entire way. *MisChief* loves these conditions and sunk her teeth into every wave that met her bow. It was effortless for her.

The Chesapeake Bay Bridge Tunnel is an engineering marvel. It has been in operation since 1964 and covers seventeen miles from shore to shore. Here, the movements of shipping traffic can be monitored and controlled in and out of the massive bay area. It also keeps enemy submarines from slipping into our waters unnoticed. Except for the bridges used by smaller fishing and motor yachts, there is only one way in and out of the bay, by navigating over the one-mile tunnels that are linked by each of the five-acre manmade islands.

The shipping traffic was heavy, and I had to stand off a bit before tacking the boat to exit the bay. A super-sized container ship loaded down with cargo was entering. She was pushing a lot of water and I wanted to give her all the room she needed.

Once outside the bay and into the Atlantic, I could see naval ships resting at Lynnhaven anchorage. It brought back memories. I had spent many days and nights anchored there on my first ship, the Ponce. It was a favorite location to conduct flight training. Helicopter pilots spent days and nights doing touch and go's off the large aft flight deck. However, on that night, there were no birds in the air; everything was quiet and still. I went below, flipped the running lights on, and came back on deck to hold a stare at the ships. I smiled and turned away.

I settled into the cockpit and fell off the breeze to a fast point of sail, a close reach. I set the autopilot for an east-southeast course, 115 true.

Numbers. You can't escape them.

LANDFALL

I t was a beautiful spring morning and still quite early. Red and I were fishing the bay. We had a fair, light breeze, and the tide was running, both of which helped us drift over a series of holes and grassy spots. The water was clear and there was a chilling bite to the air, but it would warm up fine by mid-morning.

Three minutes after tossing out the drogue to control our drift, Red caught the first fish, a nice flounder, eighteen inches. It went in the cooler with the beer. Then he caught the next five: three trout and two more flounder. Two of the trout and one of the flounder qualified for the ice treatment. I caught three bait stealers, pinfish. It was embarrassing.

As I was taking my last pinfish off the hook, Red provided valuable words of encouragement. He said, "If you don't start catching something, the network is going to cancel your fishing show and all your sponsors are going to drop you like a bad habit."

"Thanks, Red. That really helps."

Red said nothing, chuckling under his breath.

"So, I guess what you're saying is I shouldn't try to make it as a fishing guide, huh?"

"It wouldn't be something I'd recommend. That's for sure."

I said nothing.

"You don't do enough fishing, Nigel. That's all. How long have you been here now? Going on two years, maybe?"

I thought about it. *Had it been that long? Really? Time flies.*

"Man, Red. It only seems like yesterday when you and Trixie invited me to stay at your house that night. Remember?"

Red said, "That's where your recollection gets a little foggy. We didn't invite you. We didn't know what else to do with you, so we brought you home. Like a dog at the pound nobody wants. Trixie is a sucker for strays."

"Damn, Red. Do you think you could say anything else that could make me feel any better?"

Red chuckled. But it was true. It wasn't like they offered, and I accepted. We were perfect strangers the night we met. More accurately, the night they met me. Before I could lay eyes on either of them, I had slept away about thirteen hours on their couch.

The first thing I remember from that afternoon was seeing and smelling a shot of whiskey. My eyes were just opening, trying to focus against the brightness of sunshine coming through the sliding glass door. It was slow, but I took in my strange surroundings, all of it unfamiliar. Then I saw a guy with a double shot of bourbon, Jim Beam. He held it under my nose. "Hair of the dog?" he asked.

I turned my head away. A stiff shot may have made me feel better, but at that moment, it was the last thing my pounding head would accept. The room was spinning. The harsh light was hurting my eyes. I felt I was going to be sick, but fought it off. I rolled over on my back and that is when I saw a woman standing with an unlit cigarette between her fingers. She was looking over the shoulder of the guy with the whiskey. I blinked hard to bring her into focus. That's when she lit her cigarette. She took a deep draw and exhaled through her nose and said, "Morning, hotshot. Where did you blow in from?"

Even though I knew I was amongst strangers and foreign surroundings, I didn't care. I couldn't care. I didn't have the mental faculties to do so. I was horizontal. That was all I knew, that, and my going vertical wasn't an option yet.

I hadn't had a hangover like that in years and the details of how I ended up in that condition remain fuzzy. But based on what I remember, and the details I have been able to extract from my new friends, I redefined the expression *tearing up the town*.

Just twenty-four hours earlier, I was sober, tired, and the newest guy on the streets. I was transiting through to destinations unknown or not yet determined. I was in unfamiliar territory, a guy trying to start a new life, a life away from a past that would likely haunt and catch up to me.

When I sailed out of Norfolk, VA, I left nothing behind except a bad situation and a Navy life I held dear. There is no way of selecting which memories make the trip. They all come, good and bad. They're a package deal. I'm fortunate. The good ones outweigh the bad. I'm unfortunate too. The bad ones are terrible. I wasn't running or hiding, just going, not wanting to be found. There is a difference.

I sailed up from Key West after making a two-day stop at the Boca Chica Marina on the Naval Air Station. I wanted some rest. Plus, I needed to replenish my stores. After topping off with fresh diesel, taking on provisions, and filling the potable water tanks, *MisChief* and I would be ready to move on.

On my last night, I strolled into the Goat Locker, the Chief's Club, for a little Kentucky brown water; a favorite when not drinking beer. I walked straight to the bar and grabbed my favorite bar stool, number seventeen. I looked around at the others scattered about and received a protective stare from the barkeep. The Goat Locker is reserved for Chiefs and their guests. I was a stranger, so the cool reception was expected. I reached out my hand. "The name is Nigel, QMC out of Norfolk. How are you?"

He took my hand, a firm handshake. I liked him already. He maintained his grip a moment longer than usual as he squinted and studied my face. "My pleasure," he said. "The name is Steve Bales, SMC, retired. I'm the manager around here."

An SM is a signalman. The job requires a specialized skill. It is an art, all but lost in the Navy of today. They specialize in visual communication, flashing lights, semaphore, and halyard flags. That was real Navy stuff, not to be confused with all the high-tech communication gadgetry of today.

He also said he was *retired*. That was something I realized I had omitted from my introduction. I guess I should start getting used to the idea. Next time, maybe. I let it go.

I looked behind him to see what they had. The bar was well stocked. "I'll take a Woodford Reserve, neat; make it a double if you please."

I liked the way Steve worked at his bar. He reached up and grabbed an old-fashioned glass, but it wasn't clean enough for him, so he took several moments rubbing it out, polishing it with a clean bar towel. He held it up to the light, inspecting it, and then placed it in front of me with definition, anchored it to the bar with some attitude. Then he turned and grabbed the bottle off the shelf, pulled the cork, placed it in front of me, and walked away. "Pour your own, Chief. Do I have to do everything for you?"

That made me smile; it was a friendly spar from a brother in anchors. I grabbed the bottle and helped myself to a healthy, long pour. I picked up the glass, took a sniff, swirled the contents around, then took a slow sip. The aromatic burn felt wonderful as it coated the inside of my mouth and tongue, which was followed by a clean finish as it went down. I needed that.

From a bag I had with me, I pulled out several small-scale charts of the Gulf of Mexico. Where to next? That was the question. I followed the entire coastline with my finger. I studied it hard, looking at almost every waterfront town. Then I realized my finger was tapping the chart, keeping time with the classic rock playing at the bar. One song after another, good music. The commercial breaks were interesting as well, very hometown, not produced to compete in a big town market.

"Steve," I called. "What are we listening to? Which station? I might want to tune in when I get back to the boat."

"You can't tune it in down here. It's being streamed online. Oyster Radio, 106.5 on your FM dial. Comes out of Apalachicola, OysterRad io.com. Some of the guys go up there to fish. They like to listen, so I pull it up on the computer and play it from time to time. Whatever makes them happy, you know."

I studied the charts some more and wrote several possibilities before folding them up and stowing them back into the bag. I knocked back what was left of my bourbon and set the glass on the bar. I slipped a twenty under the bottle and called out a thank you to Steve as I headed to the door. He waved back.

Before I got to the door, Steve said, "Chief Logan!"

I stopped and stood there. I didn't recall exchanging last names. I turned around.

He walked up to me so nobody else could hear and said, "So, I guess if anyone comes around asking, you were never here, right?"

"I don't follow you," I said.

"Listen, Nigel. We stream a lot more than Oyster Radio around here. The guys also like to get their Navy news online from Tidewater as well. I recognized you when we shook hands."

"Oh... I see. Well, I would appreciate that," I said. "But I have nothing to hide. If somebody asks, you can be as honest as you like. I wouldn't think any less of you. If they ask you where I was headed, you can be honest there too. Tell them you don't know, because the fact is, I don't even know yet. I'm only out for a sail."

"What if they press me for a destination?" he asked.

"Come on, Chief. Do I have to think of everything for you?"

He smiled as I thought about a song I heard while sitting at the bar. A catchy tune I'd never heard before. A line from it was still running through my head.

"I tell you what, Steve. If someone is so damn bent on hearing a destination, tell them you heard me say something about Colorado... Colorado sounds nice."

We shook hands, and he stuffed my twenty-dollar bill back into my shirt pocket. "On the house," he said. "Courtesy of the Key West Chief Petty Officer's Association. Fair winds, shipmate."

"Thanks, Steve. Really."

I walked back to my boat.

It was dark early when *MisChief* and I pulled out of Key West. We had a nice broad reach, starboard tack, meaning the wind was approaching the boat from abaft the beam, or the back-right quarter. The solid 10 knots of breeze made for an easy, fast point of sail. With the autopilot on, *MisChief* tracked well. When the sun came up, I made my rounds to inspect the boat one last time to secure for sea. I wasn't expecting it to get rough, but you always expect the unexpected at sea. Secure everything.

At the navigation station, I found my laptop still open and running, eating the battery, the Oyster Radio website still on the screen. I had connected to the marina Wi-Fi when I returned to the boat. I streamed music in the salon all night long, even slept with it on. I liked the station. Now, the website was a static page, no connection, no music, no nothing. I turned the laptop off and closed the lid.

Back on deck and at the helm–I prefer to steer myself–I poured another cup of coffee from my thermos and settled in. It was nice and quiet on the outside, only the sounds of the sea and the graceful motion of a classic yacht surging along. Inside my head was a lot of noise; my mind raced from one issue to another. Thoughts of the Navy, Virginia, and what I had left behind consumed me. *MisChief* and active sailing were the therapy I needed. They would both help ease my mind.

I had gotten an excellent head start on the day, but the sun was catching up, racing toward the sky. As the shadows grew along the deck of the boat, the gorgeous blues and clarity of the Gulf of Mexico served as a grand distraction to the demons in my head. I had never sailed in the Gulf. I was an Atlantic, Chesapeake Bay kind of guy. I still love it there, always will, but this was wonderful.

I assumed my position at the helm and spent the next few days contemplating the matter at hand–the next landfall. Several times, I took the list of potential ports from my pocket and evaluated the pros and cons of each. I couldn't bring myself to a decision. I couldn't focus. The subliminal messages I had received via Oyster Radio were still ringing in my head: Port St. Joe, Indian Pass, Cape San Blas, Mexico Beach, and

Apalachicola. If I heard those locations mentioned once, I heard them a hundred times during my last night in Key West. I looked at the list one last time, studied it again. Then I shook my head, wadded it up, and stuck it back in my pocket. I sailed on.

The plan was to head west for a while, toward Mexico, until I decided. *MisChief* and I made passage past the Dry Tortugas, leaving them to starboard. Down below I was back to studying the chart, mulling it over, finger on the paper, circling the area around Cape San Blas. Then I remembered hearing Oyster Radio mention another location, one I took to describe the entire area. "The Forgotten Coast," I said it out loud, so I could hear how it sounded. I liked it.

I looked at my watch. It was morning, time to get a 1000 fix on our location. I grabbed my sexton and stood on deck; my left elbow hooked around a shroud to anchor my stance. I looked through the telescope of the sexton and found both the sun and the horizon through the mirrors and series of filters. I manipulated the index arm until the lower limb of the sun touched the horizon, three and a half nautical miles away. When I was satisfied with my measurement, I peeked at my watch and marked the time. After completing my calculations at the navigation station, I compared my findings to the GPS. I smiled; reassured once again, the GPS readings were almost as good as mine. One of these days I might gain enough trust in one of those fancy gizmos to use them exclusively, but I doubt it. I'm old school that way.

I came back on deck with a cold beer. I was feeling pretty good about myself until I noticed the sails were out of trim. They were not as ship-shape as before, and the old girl was putting up a mild protest. The wind had veered a few degrees toward *MisChief*'s stern. With the autopilot maintaining her original course, the sails were now out of trim. Not bad, but enough that *MisChief* didn't like it.

On any sailboat, if the wind shifts its direction, one of two things must happen: adjust your course to bring the trim of the sails to the new wind direction or maintain course and adjust your trim to the new wind. In her gentle protest, she was asking for one or the other.

I studied the wind shift and smiled. The new wind was favorable for what I had in mind. I reached down and cut off the autopilot, patted the tiller with my hand and said, "It's okay, girl. It's time for a fresh course, anyway. Let's go to weather."

Go to weather, meaning sail closer to the wind's actual direction. I trimmed in the main and headsail as I brought the boat toward the wind, about five degrees off a hard beat. I set the headsail first, and then I made final adjustments to the main, so they worked in concert. The helm felt perfect in my hand. The boat was very balanced, meaning I could walk away from the helm and the boat would maintain her course without my intervention. To a skipper, that is the best of feelings. I settled back in the cockpit, a light touch on the tiller. I studied the compass and applied the necessary adjustments for variation and deviation to establish our new course, 015 degrees true. What was previously due west, 270 degrees, we were now a bit better of north... north by east.

I got comfortable in the cockpit to finish my beer and to wrap my head around the long voyage ahead. My only problem was a pesky line from that new song stuck in my head. It's hard to concentrate on anything when that happens. Maybe one day I would learn the rest of it. Until then, I sang into the wind what I knew as *MisChief* pressed on, "Where to now? Well, God only knows... Colorado sounds nice..."

After a long and uneventful transit, I arrived in St. Joe Bay a little before noon at low tide. I found a nice spot out in the bay not too far away from shore. The holding looked good, so I dropped the hook. With the boat secure, it was time for some well-deserved rest that turned into a four-hour power nap. I woke up refreshed. A nice breeze was brought below by my Wind Scoop, which hung above my forward hatch. I rested there, still in motion, looking at the overhead. Then the pang hit. I was hungry and thirsty. It was time to go ashore.

I got up and took off my clothes, grabbed my ditty bag of toiletries and a towel. I stuck my head out the companionway to make sure the coast was clear. It was as clear as the beautiful water I was peering into. I spotted a large stingray under the boat, enjoying the shade of *MisChief's* shadow on the bottom. I joined him, falling in backwards, taking the Nestea Plunge. The water felt cool against my dry skin and I didn't want to get out, but the bar of soap and bottle of shampoo were calling to me from on deck. I could swim later, after I scrubbed days of salt and sweat from my body and hair.

"OMG, Red! They're fighting."

"What are you talking about, Trixie? Who's fighting?"

"Don't know."

Trixie held up her phone to show Red a picture from her Facebook feed. It was an action shot taken with a cell phone, which meant the subjects were blurry, not in focus.

"Candice posted it about 15 minutes ago," said Trixie. Then she giggled and said, "Read the caption, Red."

Red took the phone from Trixie and read the small print. *Hurry and come on out. We got music and live-action tonight. Never a dull moment at the Reid Avenue Bar and Bottle Shop.*

Red chuckled, "Nothing like a good fight to bring in the paying customers. That Candice is a smart girl."

Candice is the full-time bartender and manager of the Reid Avenue Bar and Bottle Shop in Port St. Joe. She's in her mid-to-late thirties, very attractive and single, having ditched her third husband about a year and a half ago. She has worked at the bar since graduating high school, where she was the homecoming queen two years in a row. She never went to college, but she is ruggedly smart, except when it comes to members of the opposite sex. In the relationship department, she falls a little too quickly... action without thought.

Red and Trixie were enjoying margaritas and finishing up some chile rellenos at Chico's Taqueria, the local Mexican restaurant. They were celebrating Thursday, a good day and a warm-up to the weekend. They debated on whether to drop in to check on Candice. Then the restaurant lit up like a salsa discotheque as the flashing blue lights of two squad cars filtered through the window blinds.

Red and Trixie looked at each other. The discussion was over. If for no other reason than curiosity, the desire to peek was too great. They finished their drinks, gave the local cops a chance to sort things out, paid their check, and walked out onto the sidewalk. The bar is a quick walk down and across the street.

The first thing Trixie noticed was someone sitting in the back of one of the squad cars, bloodied up pretty good. Then they saw two of the cops trying to question someone sitting on the sidewalk, hands cuffed behind his back, head hanging low. A stranger.

Trixie looked over at Red and said, "Is that Billy in the back of the car?"

"Hard to tell. Could be. He looks busted up pretty good, though."

Trixie walked over toward the car so she could get a better look, then walked back toward Red, smiling. "Yep, it's Billy alright."

Candice walked out of the bar with a couple more uniforms. They seemed to be in a fair mood. There were no telling signs of seriousness in the way they were carrying on. They walked on over to where the two other officers were trying to interview the stranger.

"He's not talking," one officer said. "He's pretty loaded."

Candice looked up and saw Red and Trixie rubbernecking from the sidewalk. She excused herself from the officers and walked over; the cops giving her skin-tight blue jeans a little too much attention as she walked away.

Red looked over toward Trixie and whispered, "I think she looks better as a blond."

"Hush your mouth, Red. She might hear you. She looks fine."

Red chuckled under his breath. Candice is known for her hair color changes. She may be a brunette one week, a redhead, or a strawberry blond the next. This week was black, jet black with a bright blue streak down the left side.

"What is going on?" asked Trixie. "What's Billy done now?"

"The jackass came in here tonight and decided he was going to make up. I haven't seen the bastard in over a year, and he shows up here drunk asking me to come back home. That he was sorry for everything. It was ridiculous."

"Come back home?" said Trixie. "Well, that's a little odd."

"Hell yeah. Tell me about it. I divorced his worthless ass over eighteen months ago and now he shows up out of the blue like everything's okay."

Candice thought for a moment and said out loud, more to herself than anyone else, "I still need to have my butt kicked for ever getting involved with his stupid ass. Live and learn."

"Well, what's his story?" asked Trixie, as she nodded toward the stranger on the curb.

"Oh! He's a keeper."

Red chuckled.

Embarrassed, Trixie gave Red a look and backhanded him across the arm.

"Never mind him, Candice. Go on."

Candice turned her head to look at the stranger for a moment. Turned back and said, "He's been in the bar since about five this afternoon. He's a real nice guy, started off with beer and later switched to bourbon. He likes his bourbon and has had a lion's share. He started a tab and paid it off three times so far. We've been talking all day and most of the night."

As Candice continued talking, all three of them walked over to where the stranger sat on the curb.

"Billy shows up already tanked and starts with his shit. When he didn't like the reception he got, he started getting hostile, like in the old days. Some bastards never change. Billy got a little rough. He grabbed and twisted my arm. Then this one here walks up, he's pretty drunk, and says, 'Buddy, you don't want to do that. Leave the lady alone.'"

Trixie said, "What happened then?"

"Well, Billy looks at him and told him to mind his own business, and this one said, 'She is my business. She's my bartender, and I always take care of my bartenders and waitresses.' Then Billy says, 'Shut your drunk hole.'

"You should have seen it, Trixie. This one here says, 'That's where you're wrong, puss. I'm not drunk. I'm just drunk enough.' Then he puckers up and blows Billy a kiss. Billy let go of my arm and went after him. That was a mistake. A big mistake. Billy got whacked on real good like. I'm sure his nose got broke. I heard it snap on the first punch. Billy went down like a rock, but you know Billy isn't real smart, so he got back up. That's when I grabbed my phone to take a picture. Billy took a couple more shots to the face before coming to rest over by the jukebox."

One cop asked, "So Candice, do you want to press charges on this guy or not?"

"No! Of course not. He did nothing. It was Billy that started all the trouble. This one here stepped in to protect me. That's all. Now take the damn cuffs off already."

Red, Trixie, and Candice watched as the cop bent down and told the stranger, "This is your lucky day, fella." As his arms went free, he looked up at the small audience and smiled. Then he found Candice and smiled more. He looked at her hard and did his best to say, "Are you alright? Is everything okay?" Then he fell backwards with his head bouncing off the sidewalk.

All excited, Candice looked at Trixie and said, "Isn't he just the sweetest thing? He's just precious?"

Red chuckled again, this time catching a cutting stare from Candice.

One cop said, "So what are you going to do with him? He can't stay here on the sidewalk. We'll have no choice but to run him in for public drunkenness."

Candice looked at Trixie. Her face spoke volumes.

Candice said, "Please. For me. I still have a few hours before I can close."

"Candice," Trixie said, "I can't take a perfect stranger in. We don't even know his name."

"His name is Nigel, Nigel Logan. Cute, huh? He was my hero tonight and I like him."

Trixie turned to Red for support. She didn't find it. Red looked back and said with a chuckle, "What? I like him too. He's a keeper!"

Trixie pulled a cigarette out of her purse and lit it. Pulled a long drag and thought about it for a few seconds and finally said, "Oh, brother! Throw his drunk ass in the back of the car."

RED SHUCKS A YARN

I t was a long day of yard work, pulling weeds and trimming shrubs amidst the heat and humidity. Keeping the grounds of The Blown Inn, my two-bedroom, one bath cottage, is a never-ending battle. It's worth the fight though if you think of it as an all-out offensive against radical Islamic terrorists. Destroy the enemy and victory is sweet.

Hydration is the key during a scorcher like this. Throughout the day, I must have poured three gallons of water into my system. But now it was time for beer amongst friends, so I grabbed a shower and shaved. Then I threw on my daily uniform: flip-flops, shorts, a Columbia fishing shirt, Calcutta sunglasses, and a visor. I jumped in my truck and headed toward Indian Pass to the Forgotten Coast Shrimp and Oyster Bar.

When I pulled up, the place was already getting crowded. The list of folks waiting to sit and eat the world's finest oysters and steamed shrimp was growing fast. I drew myself a cold draft from the keg and found my stool at the bar, number seventeen.

I got settled in and staked my claim, marking my territory: keys over here, cell phone over there, cold beer right in front of me. Once I got comfy, I heard a familiar voice from behind the bar.

"I knew you were coming, so I kept that spot open. Just for you."

I looked up. It was my buddy and often a co-conspirator of innocent controversy, Red.

"Dude," I said. "What are you doing back there?"

"Giving the boys a break. That's all. They're busting their asses tonight. Hey! Do me a favor, will ya? Take care of this." He held up his cup, rocked it back and forth. "Seeing it empty makes me sad."

I looked around. It was going to be a busy night for sure. It would be hard for the shuckers to keep up with orders. The word was out. The oysters were exceptional this week, and given the volatile harvest season in Apalachicola, it was best to *get 'em while the getting's good*. Red was lending a hand and having a few beers along the way.

We chit-chatted about this and that and told a lie or two. Then he dropped my two dozen raw oysters in front of me. I looked down at them and smiled big. They were big and beautiful. *Perfect!* The only thing missing was a fresh beer and a bottle of Crystal Hot Sauce, a problem easily remedied.

A little while later, a couple of ladies joined me at the bar, taking the two stools to my right, still toasty warm from the last inhabitants. They were first-timers and a little uncertain about the program. They sat patiently, waiting for someone to take a drink order.

I leaned over to the one next to me. "At the rate you're going, you'll be waiting all night," I said with a smile.

"Excuse me?" she said.

"All night," I said, pointing to the huge stand-up cooler against the wall. "You'll be waiting all night unless you get yourself something to drink. It's pretty much all self-service around here. Help yourself. Keep up with how much you drink and what you eat, then pay before you leave."

"Really?" They both said in perfect unison, as if they had rehearsed it a million times.

"Yes, really." Then I said, "Keep your seats. I'll get your first round, and then you're on your own. What are we having?"

I brought back a Corona and a Stella from the cooler.

Red stayed quiet and focused while we made small talk, interrupting only for the occasional refill.

Their names were Mary and Lavern. They were from a small town in North Alabama: Arab. Yes, Arab, Alabama... The little town often the brunt of many jokes by comedian Henry Cho. I guess the town actually exists. Bless their hearts.

They were staying out on the cape at the Blue Mermaid, a gorgeous, comfy place in the Cape Dunes development. I know it well. I have spilled more than a few beers on the back porch. The owners are fine folks, easy to work with and reasonable on price. They were lucky to get that unit.

I was answering their questions about the area as best I could, making a few recommendations here and there. It was going great, and I was nursing my last four or five oysters, when what happened next almost killed me.

Mary said, "We've noticed several of the homes out here have large mounds directly in front of them. Not all of them, just some. I'm sure you know what I'm talking about, right? They each appear to be about the same size and shape. What are they?"

I held up one finger to show I needed a moment. I was in the middle of washing down an oyster, and the last thing I wanted to be thinking of, at that moment, was a septic tank.

Coastal regions are notorious for having groundwater levels that are extremely close to the earth's surface. This makes the installation of conventional underground septic systems impossible. The danger of tapping into or contaminating groundwater systems is too great with a regular system, so they place septic tanks and their associated drain fields surface in earth mounds.

I was about ready to explain. But, during swallowing, I heard Red say, "Ancient Indian burial mounds."

My head ducked, and I gasped, sucking the oyster and beer right down my windpipe. I couldn't believe what I had just heard. I was in trouble and about to die, right then and there. Half laughing and half crying, I was drowning in a sea of oysters and beer.

It almost seems fitting, taking my last breath on number seventeen, but I wasn't ready to go, not yet. I had plenty of fight left in me, and it took everything I could muster to keep from spewing everything from my mouth and lungs back out onto the bar. It was tough, but I pulled through with a little slap on the back from Mary, and a bit of encouragement from Red. "Hang in there, buddy", he said. "Stay with me. Keep away from the bright light. Don't look at it. Come back. Stay with me now. You still owe me twenty bucks."

That did it, along with one last slap from Mary. With my eyes awash and an air passage partially open, I hacked the audible, "Twenty bucks! What twenty bucks?"

Chuckling, Red said, "I thought that would bring you round."

Lavern brought me a fresh beer to clear my throat and polish my recovery. Still a little moist in the lungs, I gurgled, "Ladies. Let me introduce you to my buddy, Red."

Red grunted, "Howdy."

Mary said, "So, Red. You were saying... about the Indian burial mounds and all?"

Red gazed over at me with stone-cold seriousness. It was a look with a message. I picked up on it immediately. Shut up. Don't say a word. Let me have this one. I got it.

I smiled and gave him a little intro. "Yes, Red. Please. You know the history of this so much better than I do. Enlighten us."

He put down his shucking knife, took a long pull from his solo cup, and handed it to me for a refill. He leaned up against the counter and said, "Those are not ordinary Indian burial mounds. They're enchanted, full of positive spirits, and coveted as good luck by those that have one."

"They contain the remnants of an extinct people, the Septicoles, a mix of the Porenyafeka and Yurenchabuket clans of southern Georgia. They were an agrarian people that settled this area to expand their livelihood to include fishing. It was a decision that would ultimately be their demise."

How he did that with a straight face, God only knows how. I had to bite the inside of my mouth. I looked over at the ladies. They seemed to buy it. Red was selling it damn well, like a silver-tongued used car salesman.

"And you say they're good luck?" asked Laverne.

"Yep. Legend has it, great fortuitous events befall those that own one. Hell, Stan Kastin, he has a mound out by Money Bayou. His wife cashed in big at bingo last weekend. Three of her cards hit at the same time. Brought home 97 dollars and 14 cents, she did. And Jerry Blanton, he has a mound out on Indian Pass. Yesterday, he bought an old paperback for seventy-five cents at the Goodwill. It had a fifty-dollar bill folded up and tucked inside. I call that pretty damn lucky."

"Gosh," I said. "How could anybody get any luckier?"

"I'll tell you how," Red replied. "You know Pam Bridges, right?"

"Sure. She's married to Steve. Fine fella."

"Right."

I looked over at Mary and Lavern. "Steve and Pam," I said. "They live down the street a short piece, back toward Port St. Joe. The big yellow place on the right, right before the curve. Their mound is huge, a double, but in the backyard."

"So, what's up with Pam?" I asked.

Red leaned over closer. Lowered his voice a bit and said, "She took an EPT pregnancy test last week and the stick popped a big blue minus sign, a negative test, not pregnant."

"So why does that make her so damn lucky?" I asked.

"Because she's been copulating with Steve's brother, that's why."

"Ned?" I said. "I thought he was still in jail for mullet poaching."

"He was, but he's been out for about three months now. They've been going at it pretty regular since."

"And how is it you came across this juicy little piece of local intelligence?" I asked.

"Well. Ned was over at..."

Laverne interrupted, "Too much information, guys. T.M.I., T.M.I." She paused for a second to look at Mary and said, "Damn. And I thought women were bad for back-fence talking."

"Sorry 'bout that," I said. "I guess we got a little sidetracked."

"So, what happened to the Indians? Were they destroyed by a rival tribe or something?" Mary asked.

"On the contrary," said Red. "They were a kind and peaceful people. Didn't really have any enemies at all. Legend has it, it was the seafood. Poor souls should have left well enough alone and stayed in Georgia to live on peanuts. They all had an inherent gene and were allergic to shellfish. They didn't figure it out until it was too late. The shrimp got them."

"Wow," said Laverne. "That really is an incredible story."

"You're telling me," I said.

Red cut me a look, catching the sarcasm in my tone. I guess the ladies did, too. Laverne looked down the bar and asked me, "So you don't believe in the legend? You don't feel the mounds are full of good luck and fortune?"

I sat there for a moment and thought about how I could best answer without discrediting my friend. He had put so much creative energy into his story. Then it hit me.

"I don't place a lot of faith into legends and such," I said. "Call me a skeptic if you like, but I can't buy into the whole spiritual fascination of the Indian burial mound thing. Personally," I paused for a moment, took a sip of beer and said. "I think they're full of shit."

Red growled under his breath and said, "Typical pagan unbeliever."

I smiled and finished my oysters and beer.

A Little Something from the Keys

I was finishing up a miserable morning of fishing from underneath the big bridge on Highway 98. There's nothing worse than not catching a thing while everyone around you is getting their limit and then some. It's very frustrating. To hell with this!

I was packing my gear in the back of my truck and closing the tailgate when my phone rang. I looked at the screen. It was my buddy, Red. I looked back over my shoulder at the five fellas still fishing, each with a fish on. *Screw you guys!*

"Good morning and thanks for calling *Everything but Catching Fish Charters*. We're fishing, not catching. How can I help you?"

"Uh oh," said Red. "Sounds like another unlucky day with the hook."

Being unlucky has nothing to do with it. I just have the toughest time getting a fish to take my bait. Basically, I suck at fishing. I love doing it and the challenge. *But damn!* Let me catch a decent fish from time to time. That's all I want.

I rolled my eyes. "Yeah. Unlucky. That's it. Piss poor luck. I keep it in my tackle box, spray a little on every bait. Wouldn't go fishing without it." I paused a moment and asked, "Wait a minute. When did ya'll get back into town?"

Red, his wife Trixie, and a fistful of others went down to Key West for a little escape vacation. They love to people-watch, so they picked the week of Fantasy Fest and weren't disappointed. The exhibitionists were in full disclosure mode. It's so crazy during that week, even *strange* is considered lame. If you've ever wondered how wacky people can be, go to Key West during Fantasy Fest. It makes Mardi Gras in New Orleans look like a mortician's convention.

Some folks go down there to escape the normalcy of life and let go. They wish to throw all caution and inhibitions to the wind, to get caught up in the bizarre. Once Monday rolls around it's time to clean all the evidence of debauchery off their phones and cameras and return to the mainstream of reality. The kids will never get to see those pictures of grandma's full body paint job, or grandpa dancing in his feather g-string in the middle of Mallory Square. *Thank goodness.*

In stark contrast to the visitors looking for a good time are the scores living the dream every day, the actual fantasy freaks. To them, the festival never ends. That's kind of scary, especially when you consider their potential to breed and right to vote. But that's one of the great things about America. I think.

"We got in late last night," Red answered. "The flight got delayed, but I can tell you about that some other time. Come on over to the house later. Trixie is whipping up some greens, and we have a huge ham that needs to disappear. Plus, I have a little something for you, a memento from the island."

Now, when you get an invitation to dine on some of Trixie's greens, you don't turn it down. I always used to hate greens. It didn't matter which kind. They could be turnip, collard, or mustard greens. The thought of them turned my stomach. It stems from my grade school days and the greens the lunchroom ladies served up about four times a week. It didn't matter how hungry I was, there was no way I could bring myself to eat that shit. Then I got shamed into trying Trixie's. *Damn! What have I been missing all these years?* They are the best.

"Yummy! I'll bring beer," I said.

Red and Trixie have a beautiful place out on Cape San Blas overlooking the Gulf of Mexico. They've done well for themselves, but neither has a pretentious bone in their body. They are regular, hard-working folks, respected by everyone on the Forgotten Coast. It is tough to find anyone around here that doesn't know them, and it's even tougher to find someone that doesn't like them. Their vocations probably have something to do with that.

Trixie works closely inside the local justice system and Red is a respected educator of higher learning. Together, they've been able to pool their talents and resources to create a professional partnership that has touched the lives of many within the community.

She owns and operates Trixie's Freedom Bail Bonds, and he runs a complementary business serving as the headmaster of Red's Institute for Drunk Drivers or RIDD for short. The two operations are like them, meant for each other. They go together like salt and water. Trixie bails them out for DUI; Red enrolls them for a new class the next. It is nothing short of genius.

When I got to their house, I saw someone leaving. It was Little Bit. He had a big container of greens and an all too familiar international orange t-shirt.

It's a customary part of Trixie's service to provide each customer with a complimentary shirt. The front says **I Got My Freedom at Trixie's!** The phone number is on the back.

Little Bit's real name is Luther Collins. He works the shrimp boats out of Port St. Joe. And there is nothing *little* about him. He's a big boy at about six foot, two inches, 225 lbs, and muscle-bound. He's a good guy and an honest, hard worker. There was a time when he was no stranger to trouble, but that was during his days of heavy drinking. But, as I understood it, he hadn't had a drink in years, so it surprised me to see him fleeing the house with a shirt.

I tried to stop him as he was walking to his truck, but he waved me off, saying, "I can't right now. Too much to do. We'll talk later." He jumped in and drove away in his rusty old Toyota 4 by 4; an old, faded bumper sticker on the back window that says *My Wife is a 2007 Honor Grad from RIDD, Port St. Joe.* I smiled.

I grabbed my cooler, made my way to the door, and let myself in. Red and Trixie were already sitting on the back porch, taking in the view of the Gulf. I opened the sliding glass door. "Knock! Knock!"

"Nigel! Come on out and grab a seat," said Red. "The surf's really up this afternoon."

"Thanks," I said. "I saw Little Bit leaving with a shirt. What's up?"

Trixie answered, "Can't say. Confidentiality, you know. The whole right-to-privacy thing."

Red said, "Trixie can't say anything, but I can."

"Was he drunk?"

"Nope. I don't think Little Bit has had a drink in five or six years."

Trixie said, "Red, tell him about the naked part. That's my favorite."

"So much for confidentiality," Red replied. "Anyway, yesterday driving home after work, Little Bit spots some mullet jumping in the surf. He whips over to the side of the road and grabs his cast net, lands 23 mullet in three throws."

"Damn!" I said. "Twenty-three. That made for a quick haul." I paused a bit and said, "Hey, when are you going to teach me to throw a net? You said you would."

"Teach you? You... throw a cast net?" Red chuckled and said, "Wouldn't do any good. You can't catch shit as it is."

"Thanks for the vote of confidence, Red."

Trixie piped in again and said, "Finish the story, Red. Get to the street fight."

Red looked at Trixie and said, "Are you telling this story or me?"

"You know I can't say anything," Trixie answered. "Just wouldn't be right."

Red took a moment to give Trixie a blank stare before continuing, "Anyway, Little Bit gets his cooler of mullet home and leaves it on his back porch. He lives over in Mexico Beach, you know. After showering, he steps out of the bathroom..." Red smiled and chuckled. "And he sees these two guys running and making off with his cooler and mullet."

"Oh no," I said. "This can't be good."

"Shhhh! Shhh!" said Trixie. "He's getting to my favorite part."

Red continued, "Well, Little Bit wastes no time. He hit that screen door in full stride, wearing nothing but some leftover water from the shower. By the time he hit the lawn, the two thieves were already pulling away in their car, Little Bit's mullet and cooler in the back seat. Little Bit, he doesn't slow down any. The chase was on."

Trixie added with her husky laugh, "It was a full monty pursuit. I can see it now, parts flipping and flopping everywhere. He didn't even stop to put on sunscreen. I would have paid money to see that."

I said, "But certainly Little Bit knew he couldn't outrun the car. The thieves had to be long gone in no time."

"Under normal circumstances, no," said Red, "but we're not talking normal here, especially with Little Bit's determination to get his mullet back. Little Bit never slowed down and cut every corner of every lawn in the chase. And while he knew damn well, he couldn't run down the car. What he knew was the thieves couldn't outrun the tourist traffic. When he caught up with them, they were moving at a snail's pace on Highway 98. That's when things got ugly. Those two didn't fare well."

"The tourists got their money's worth," said Trixie. "That's for sure."

Red concluded, "When the MBPD got to the scene, all they found was a tired, old Ford Focus. It was blocking traffic, still running in the middle of the street. Then they found two unconscious individuals sprawled out on the side of the road. The cops later caught up with Little Bit. They found him taking an unhurried stroll down the highway toward his house, his cooler covering up all the important parts. Later, he called Trixie, and I went out there to get him out of the joint."

"Wait... wait," I said. "I heard about this. They reported it on Oyster Radio on the drive over here. They mentioned Little Bit's actual name, but it went in one ear and out the other."

Trixie said laughing, "I wonder if they found anything when they frisked him, patted him down?"

We all laughed at the thought of that until Red changed the subject, "Alright. Alright. Enough of that, already. Nigel, come with me. I got something in the car for you." I got up and followed him toward the steps leading off the deck.

Trixie objected. First, she spoke to me, "Nigel. Don't go round there with him." Then she pleaded with Red, "Red! No. Please do not give that damn thing to him. It's awful. Red! Oh my God. This is so embarrassing."

Red chuckled under his breath as we walked.

When Red told me they were heading to Key West, I was immediately envious. I wanted to go. After leaving Norfolk, VA on *MisChief*, I made a small provisioning stop at the naval base there, but I hadn't been on Greene, Duval, or any of the other streets of Key West in years. So, when they sojourned there, I had only one request. I asked Red to have a beer for me at Capt. Tony's Saloon. He said, "Seems easy enough. No problem."

Sometimes, things are never that easy.

While they were gone, I moved into a small house in town, a cottage actually—a place known as The Blown Inn. I rented it from a couple out of north Georgia. It was a first for me. I hadn't lived in a house since I left my parents' place to join the Navy. I've always stayed on boats, either on my ship or on one of my many sailboats.

I had little stuff, so moving didn't take long at all. Getting the utilities and phone hooked up took more time than I would have thought. I stood in the small living room and looked around. It felt weird, but it felt right, like I belonged there. Then the phone rang. And when I say rang, that's exactly what I mean. The house came with an old vintage rotary phone with actual moving parts. The clappers were smacking the crap out of the bells inside.

I looked at the phone and thought, *Here we go. The first of a long series of wrong numbers.* I hoped the last person who had this number didn't owe a bunch of money. I picked up the phone. It was Red.

"I'm on stool seventeen. I'm having your beer now. Actually, it may be your second."

"Red, how are you guys doing?" I paused and thought... "Wait a minute. How the hell did you get this number? They only hooked it up about two hours ago."

"Aww... Ancient Chinese secret," Red said in the worst East Asian accent I'd ever heard.

"No. Really. How did you get my number so fast?"

Red continued with his bad accent, "Little sister work at Mama-san Bell. She knows people that know things. Keep big brother in loop."

I shook my head with a smile. We chatted about this, that, and all the other. They were having a great time. There was a lot of roaming, people-watching, good food, and plenty of libations. We talked about my move and other casual chit-chat. Then he asked, "Hey! Would you be interested in a print of the saloon, a picture of Capt. Tony's, something to hang in the cottage?"

It sounded like a great idea. The place was empty, naked, so having a little something to hang on the walls would be great. "That would be cool, but you don't have to do that. You've completed your mission, beers at Capt. Tony's."

"It will be my pleasure," he said.

We said our goodbyes and hung up.

Their stay on the island was ending. It was the last day and Red had not yet found the perfect print. He considered various mediums, from photo prints to production art by various local artists. He couldn't find the right rendition of the world-famous bar. Not happy with what was available, he went the extra-special mile. He would commission an artist to produce a piece to his liking, something special and meaningful. He's a sensitive guy like that.

A cooler in one hand and a beer in the other, Red roamed around and interviewed several local artists and vetted their abilities to complete such a project in the brief time available. Over more beers, he reviewed samples of their work. He wanted to make sure the artist he picked could not only paint a picture of the famous watering hole but also capture the essence of the historic establishment. Red does nothing half-ass.

He finally settled on a sidewalk artist named Jean Paul. It seems all the artists down there go by that name. The artist promised he could paint anything and in short order. Red gave him a picture he had taken earlier that morning.

"Yes." Jean Paul said, "Capt. Tony's. Of course, of course," he assured. The artist won points with his bad, fake French accent. Red liked that about him. "I can paint this. I've brought it to life on canvas many, many times before. This I would love to do this for you. All I need is an hour and my usual fee."

With his red solo cup now showing all white on the inside, and time running out, Jean Paul got the job. Red looked at his watch and told him he had three hours.

"Oui. Oui," replied Jean Paul.

Red chuckled as he walked away thinking, *Oui, Oui, Oui, Oui... all the way home*. He continued his roaming.

Red opened the back hatch of his Ford Explorer, or *Exploder*, as he likes to call it. He reached in and pulled out the artwork. We could still hear Trixie from the deck, pleading one last time, "Red! Please!"

"Here it is," he said.

We both stood there looking at it. I smiled. He chuckled. It was perfect.

Looking at it, I told him, "This is great, dude! Perfect. Thanks." I meant every word. We looked at each other and laughed.

"So why is Trixie making such a fuss?"

"I don't know," he said. "I feel she thinks it lacks a certain polished, artistic quality. That it's missing some level of perfection, making it unsuitable for display. Like it doesn't quite measure up."

"I don't know," I said. "Look at the reality in the depth of field, how the light seems to cast over the roof, the dimensions, the angles. The colors make the piece jump right out at you. The realism is overwhelming. I think it's superb."

It was none of those things. We had both seen better kindergarten art. There is no shortage of starving artists that do fabulous work. You can find talent everywhere, but that Jean Paul would make it, even as a starving artist, was a dream. I have seen art that, to me, looked bad, but to others looked fabulous. Even in those pieces, I could appreciate the artistic expression put into the work, but not in Jean Paul's rendition of Capt. Tony's Bar. The painting was a comedy, and for that reason alone made it even more special.

We both gazed at the work in wonder. Then I said, "The guy doesn't appear to be a very strong speller. He misspelled saloon three different ways."

"Yeah, I noticed that myself. It was the first piece I've ever commissioned. I didn't realize I should have gotten an artist with a spellchecker. My mistake. Live and learn."

I told him, "Well, I love it anyway. Thanks again." I gave him a big hug as we laughed and chuckled. I let him go, and said, "Let's go get a beer, my friend."

We joined Trixie back on the deck. She was leaning forward, face in her hands.

A RANSOM FOR MAXINE

I first heard the news from Luke McKenzie himself. I was jogging through town when I became overcome with the urge for a cold, scratch'n beer. A scratch'n beer. You get an itch; you scratch. I had completed over three miles of my run when I passed the Reid Avenue Bar and Bottle Shop in downtown Port St. Joe. The sight of the place tickled my throat, so I slowed down to a walk and laced my fingers behind my head. I stopped and turned around. My skin was slick with a combination of sweat and sea salt picked up from the coastal air. I opened the door to the bar and took a vicious shiver as the air conditioning rushed out to meet my overheated body. Then I strolled on in.

Old Man McKenzie was sitting alone at the bar. He was staring at his beer, which was now warm, the mug frost long since dried and gone. Stool seventeen was right next to him.

Luke McKenzie is a gentle, good-natured, elderly man, probably in his late seventies or early eighties. I've never asked. You wouldn't know it by his appearance. He's well preserved. He lives alone, surviving off his Navy pension, social security, and what little he earns with his small lawn care business.

"Luke," I said. "Your beer is growing a beard. Can I get you a fresh one?"

He turned his head toward me, his eyes filled with worry and distress. "They took her, Nigel," he said. "She's gone. They have my Maxine."

"What?" I said. "What are you talking about? Who has Maxine?"

"I wish I knew," he said and slid a letter toward me.

It was a ransom note, short and sweet, using cut-out letters to spell the words. I immediately recognized some letters as being from advertisements out of a local rag, The Oyster. It is a small, free publication catering to the tourist crowd and serves as a complement to my favorite FM radio station, 106.5 Oyster Radio.

If you wanna see your deer Maxine alive, you will need to get together about $1,500 to set her free. We will contact you later with more instructions.

Stapled to the letter was a color picture printed out on plain paper. It was of Maxine with yesterday's newspaper, *The Star*, held under her chin by one of her captors.

I read the note a couple more times. *We will contact you.* That told me there was more than one involved. They misspelled dear and weren't specific about the amount of ransom. About $1,500? And there were some things about the picture that caught my eye. Without a doubt, these kidnappers are a bunch of knuckleheads.

"Luke. Have you taken this to the police?" I asked.

He shook his head in disappointment and said, "They didn't take it seriously. They laughed at me and called it the great "KID"-napping caper. I argued, but they said they had more important matters to tend to. Told me to call the FBI. That they handle cases like this."

The Great "KID"-napping caper. That was pretty clever. I almost laughed myself but didn't want to offend or be disrespectful to Luke in his hour of crisis. But it was funny. After all, Maxine is a goat.

Luke, or Old Man McKenzie as he is affectionately known, and Maxine have been together for years. They have been local icons long before I arrived on the Forgotten Coast. You rarely see one without the other. Maxine is probably the smartest damn goat in the world and serves as cheap labor to Luke's little lawn care endeavor. While Luke mows, Maxine trims around the trees and structures, eating down to the ground areas the mower can't reach. It's the damnedest thing you've ever seen, and she knows exactly what to do. She's like a four-legged weed-eater with horns and a beard.

"The FBI," I said. "That actually might not be a bad idea. Have you called them yet?"

"Hell No! I haven't called the FBI. What? Do you think I'm crazy? You know how I feel about the damn Federal Government. I want them to stay the hell out of my life, so I damn sure ain't going to invite them in."

Luke isn't fond of the Feds. A few years ago he got audited by the IRS for some questionable expenses on his business tax returns. In particular, the 1099 Miscellaneous, the report sent to the IRS each year to report monies paid to contractors.

It is a common error of some businesses, especially small ones, to misclassify actual employees as contractors. Often the error results from questionable advice provided by a best friend's, cousin's, sister's boyfriend that runs an accounting business from the back seat of a 1984 Chevy Caprice station wagon, a spray-painted sign on the door: "Anytime-Anywhere Tax Service." I think you get the idea.

The error is sometimes more than a mistake; it is intentional. There are significant cost savings associated with having contractors over em-ployees. Contractors don't qualify for benefits and there is no additional employer matching for Social Security and Medicare withholdings. For some, the allure of saving a few bucks in the wake of twisting the rules is too great.

This was why the IRS investigated Luke. Questions about the validity of his contract labor had popped up on their radar. They sent various notices and questionnaires in the mail. Luke ignored all of them, includ-ing one announcing a date for an actual site visit.

The agent's arrival wasn't met with a kind reception.

The examiner wasn't there to go over Luke's entire tax return, only the details surrounding the 1099 contract labor. He wouldn't look any further unless something else presented itself during the review. Had

Luke properly completed the 1099 each year, the IRS wouldn't have had any reason to be sitting at his kitchen table.

Agent Castor, badge no. 5789653, was from the Tallahassee field office. He was a young man, mid-thirties, medium build with a strong chin and an even stronger smile despite Luke's unpleasant deportment.

"Mr. McKenzie," the young agent started. "I'm so sorry for the intrusion. We tried to handle this through the mail, but, for whatever reason, we were unsuccessful."

Luke sat stoic and silent; arms crossed in a full display of defiance. A pile of unopened letters from the IRS was on the kitchen counter, mixed with the occasional credit card offer. If Agent Castor saw them when he came into the kitchen, he gave no indication.

"Mr. McKenzie, the reason we want to talk to you is the improper completion of your 1099s for one of your contractors."

"There you go," Luke said. "You haven't been here five minutes and you've already started with your damn lies. Let's try the truth for once, or is that too much to ask?"

"Excuse me?"

"The truth, dammit. You said contractors, plural. I ain't got but one. You're trying to make this into some capital case, ain't cha boy?"

Agent Castor looked back down at his notes and shuffled through a few pages, then looked up, embarrassment written all over his face. He said, "Please forgive me, Mr. McKenzie. You are absolutely right. I certainly did not mean to insinuate anything. One 1099. It says so right here."

Luke relaxed a little. He took great comfort in putting the young agent on the defensive. He was in the driver's seat... for a minute anyway.

"Mr. McKenzie, we have questions surrounding the reporting of your one contractor." Agent Castor put a little extra emphasis on the word *one.* "You have been reporting 1099 income for the same individual for the past several years with all zeroes as their Social Security Number or SSN. Plus, the fact he or she..."

"She," Luke said, interrupting the young agent.

"Very well then," said agent Castor. "We need to clear up this SSN business. Plus, since she has been working for you so long, we need to determine her actual status. She could be an employee as opposed to a contractor. Often, a simple oversight in classifying the services of the help."

"It sounds to me you've already made up your damn mind, boy," said Luke.

"No, sir. Not at all. We need to collect all the facts first, like the SSN issue. Does she or doesn't she have a Social Security Number?"

"Nope."

"Really. Is she an illegal alien? Don't worry; we're not so much concerned with her immigration status. That's for the Department of Homeland Security to vet through. And we don't openly share any information with them."

"Nope," Luke said again with a grin, shaking his head. "Illegal alien? Why, if that isn't the dumbest and thing I've ever heard. She was born right here in Gulf County, twenty miles up the road in Wewa. *Pronounced* "Wewah," short for Wewahitchka.

Agent Castor was now getting a little frustrated. His courteous professionalism was wearing thin.

"So, if she isn't an alien, then why doesn't she have a Social Security Number?"

"Well, that would be stupid, wouldn't it? She doesn't qualify for one."

"She doesn't? Why is that?"

"Because she's a goat, you idiot!"

"A goat?"

"That's what I said, son, 'a goat.'"

"A goat can't have a Social Security Number!"

"Then you would agree with me?"

"Agree with you about what?"

"That it would be pretty damn stupid to give a Social Security Number to a goat!"

Things went downhill from there.

I was kidding about calling the FBI. That would have been dumb, but I needed to feel him out. If he was thinking about it, I would want to intervene. I wouldn't want him to do anything stupid or embarrassing.

"Okay, you're right," I said. "Calling the FBI wouldn't be the best of ideas. This probably needs to be handled internally, without the authorities. Sometimes the legalities of things get in the way."

"That's what I was thinking. Will you help me?" he asked.

"I'll do what I can. I can't promise anything, but I think we can figure this thing out. Sit tight, go home, get some rest, and let me work on a few things. If you get any new ideas, call me."

I left him there at the bar. I stood up and pulled a sweaty, folded over twenty out of my pocket. I gave it a spinning fling toward Candice, the barkeep. "Give him a fresh one, and this is for his tab. Don't let him drive if he's not fit to do so."

"Do you think you know who did it?" Candice asked.

"I'm not sure. At this point, it's all speculation. I have ideas, but that's about all. Will you call me if you should hear anything come across the bar?"

She gave me a smile and a nod. I was almost to the door when she stopped me. "Hey, Nigel."

I turned around.

"Thanks for coming in." With a wink and subtle lick of her upper lip, she added, "And for wearing those shorts."

I rolled my eyes as I turned and walked out the door.

I got home and took a shower, nice and hot; cooled steam dripped from the mirror and ceiling. I toweled off, put on a pair of cargo shorts, and grabbed a cold beer out of the fridge. I sat out on my front porch under the ceiling fan, no shirt. I thought for a bit, then chuckled. *The Great "KID"-napping*. The local cops were funny but unprofessional. They should have shown a bit more respect and saved the humorous comments for locker room antics.

I took a sip of beer and considered the goofy ransom note, the picture, and the situation. These guys are either dumb and want to get caught, or the whole thing is nothing more than a bad joke. My bet was on the latter, but how far were they willing to take it? That was the question. All I knew was the old man was at wit's end and needed help.

The picture provided much in the form of evidence. There was the great shot of the captor's hand: skinny, bony fingers holding the newspaper under Maxine's chin, complete with a clear view of a senior class ring. From under a magnifying glass I could read, Port St. Joe High, Class of 2010.

Then there was the background scenery and the angle of the shot. The camera had been low enough that it allowed for plenty of sky and treetops. Not any treetops though, these were treetops I had seen before. They were signature treetops with two big nests near each other, resting in the top of two old dead hardwoods. I couldn't place where I had seen them. *Damn.* It was driving me crazy.

I also considered some of the potential problems our kidnappers might face. The first being, where would you best hide a goat, especially one that was sure to be pissed off?

Maxine is spoiled. She lives in the house with Luke and has her very own bedroom. She has her favorite television shows: *Duck Dynasty*, *The Voice*, and *Project Runway*. Luke has never figured that last one out, but it's what she likes. And she has a couple of cans of cold beer before bed. As it goes for goats, she is used to living the Life of Riley. Anything out of the ordinary would undoubtedly set her off.

I took another sip and closed my eyes. I thought about the picture and the nests. It was making more sense, and I eliminated several locations. I couldn't nail down the one spot I had floating around somewhere in my mind.

I was putting together a few good ideas when I heard my back screen door open, an unmistakable squeal. My eyes opened. The spring of the door slammed it shut, bouncing free against the frame. I heard the unmistakable sound of my refrigerator opening, then closing. Heavy footsteps were crossing my hardwood floor, then the unmistakable sound of carbonation escaping a bottle of beer. The top quickly twisted off.

"I'm out on the porch."

I looked over my shoulder to see my buddy Red standing in the door-way, a blank look on his face. "Come on out," I said. "Grab yourself a seat."

He stood there for a moment or two and said, "Dang!"

He took a seat on the swing.

"What's the matter?"

Red took a long pull from the beer, released a refreshing gasp and said, "Ah, yeah. Man, that is cold. You must have the coldest beer in town."

"You mean I had the coldest beer in town. That was my last one."

Red wasn't too far from the truth. If it isn't the coldest beer around, it's damn near. My refrigerator is from the early fifties. It's old-school with a latching door, probably the original unit that came with the house.

They outlawed such refrigerators in 1956 because of their danger to children. It's a classic and works a little too well. It either cools to perfection or over-compensates. More and more these days, I'm waking up to half-frozen provisions. If I keep my beers toward the front of the box, they will stay above freezing, the perfect temp. I can deal with a little frozen milk, but the minute I lose one beer to an over-zealous refrigerator, the door comes off its hinges and off to the dump it goes.

"What's bothering you, Red?"

"It's frustrating, that's all," he said.

"What is it?"

"It's this CRS, that's what. It seems to be getting worse, and it's driving me crazy. Seems to be flaring up especially bad these days... Anyway, I came over to bring you something, but..."

"Whoa, Whoa, Whoa, Buddy. Slow down," I said. "Don't change the subject on me. What's with this CRS stuff? Is it serious, contagious?"

"Well, it can be, I guess," he said. "It all depends on the circumstances. That's what I was trying to tell you. I came over to bring you something, but I left it at the house."

"I'm not following."

"Damn, Nigel. This is embarrassing enough without you making it worse. I left it at the house. I forgot it, okay? It's the damn CRS: Can't Remember Shit!"

I shook my head. "Ah hell, Red. You ain't right. Forget about all that for now. You can give it to me later. We're going for a boat ride. Come on."

"But we're out of beer," he said.

"Red, as long as the CVS drug store is open, we'll never be out of beer." He smiled.

I had bought an old powerboat, a Key West 1700, center console. I call it *Chum Bucket*. It's powered by a 90hp Johnson outboard, which I affectionately refer to as Johnny. I bought it as a platform for an idea that I had been tossing around. When I retired from the Navy, I wasn't ready to retire. To have my druthers, I'd still be steaming along on some rusty warbird in the middle of the Mediterranean. But it didn't work out that way; those plans got cut off early. In the end, I still wasn't ready to retire. I wasn't prepared to don a pair of sexy Rockport shoes, sport an old ship's cap, and daily walk the corridors of some Panama City Mall. I needed something to do, something to occupy my mind and time.

There is little occupational opportunity in Port St. Joe, so if I was going to do something, I was going to have to create something for myself. I turned to a side passion, photography. I'm a sailor of boats, and I like them, love them actually. I love sailboat racing. I did plenty while in Norfolk. I figured, why not travel around as a regatta photographer, shoot boats, and peddle my work to the skippers and crew? *Chum Bucket* would serve as the perfect platform to work a racecourse and the boats.

Chum Bucket also serves as the perfect boat to play in St. Joe Bay. She is small and fast. If I needed to get somewhere quick, she can make short work of it, but at a significant cost. When you open the horses in Johnny, the old girl gets mighty thirsty and ethanol-free gas isn't cheap. I was reminded of that as Red topped off the tank at the Exxon station.

As promised, we swung by the CVS to recharge the cooler with ice and beer before heading to the boat ramp to launch. We lucked out. There was no wait. We splashed, parked, and had the girl fired up and easing out into the channel in no time. And as quick, Red began working on the ballast transfer operation, moving one beer at a time from the cooler to his personal holding tank.

"You want one?"

"No thanks," I said. "After a while, maybe."

"Where we headed?"

"I don't know. The tide is running. I thought we might drift the channel behind Pig Island and get a line wet. Catch some dinner. A little fresh fish in the belly sounds good."

That wasn't altogether a lie. I needed to catch something to eat, and a big speckled trout on the grill sounded damn good. It would also give me a chance to pay attention to the tree line.

"Oh, is that why you brought me? Who's going to do the catching? You can't fish for shit."

"Thanks, Red."

It was true. I would starve if I had to rely on catching my own fish for survival. Some days were better than others, but, more often than not, I spent more time cleaning other people's fish than my own. Sad, but true.

We were about an hour and a half past high tide. The water this far back in the bay gets thin, so, with a falling tide, I had to be careful. We were on a nice easy plane, zipping along toward the back of the bay and the south end of Pig Island when Red gave my heart a start. "Put it back, dammit! Put it back. Let it go!"

"Damn, Red. What is it? You scared the shit out of me."

"The son of a bitch is going to keep it, Nigel. He caught a trout. It's too small, and he hasn't turned it loose. You know the rule, a fifteen-inch minimum," he said.

Red barked one last time. "Did you hear me? You bastard! I said to let it go! Play by the damn rules." Red took a drink of beer, stood next to me at the helm station, and chuckled.

I was confused. I looked around and couldn't see any fishermen, none close enough to see their catch, anyway. I scanned around and almost asked him what in the hell he was talking about when it caught my eye. There it was, flying low across the water but gaining height. An osprey, in its talons was a trout, head pointing forward for aerodynamics. It was a catch too small for humans, but big enough to serve as a raptor snack.

I watched as it gained altitude, heading toward the island. I cut the wheel to follow, then checked the depth. Then told Red to hold on to something other than his beer. I leaned on Johnny to give chase.

Red looked at me, and over his signature chuckle, said, "You're wasting your time. He won't drop it for you either."

I looked over and smiled as the boat ran wide open. There was little wind, so the water was flat, making for a nice ride. We were catching up, and for the first time since leaving the dock, there was something on board drinking faster than Red. Johnny was doing a number on the liquid dinosaurs in the tank.

After a while, I felt the bottom of the bay through my bare feet. The water was getting thin and it would only continue to get worse the closer I got to the island. I trimmed the motor up a bit to keep the prop from mowing the seagrass, a fragile part of the bay's ecosystem. Plus, a good boat prop isn't cheap, nor is the lower end of a motor.

Through my polarized sunglasses, I could see it was going to get worse quick. I told Red to hold on. He squeezed his beer tight as I quickly throttled back and trimmed the motor up even more.

At idle and the boat in neutral, I grabbed my binoculars and found the bird. Its wings were still flapping hard, gaining height with every powerful stroke. As I followed the bird of prey through the air, Red said, "Does he still have it?"

I didn't answer and kept tracking the bird. I saw its destination and adjusted the binoculars for better focus. It was a nest, and in it his partner was patiently waiting. I watched as the proud fella landed on the edge. She seemed to be a little miffed, raising hell, like he'd been out all hours of the night drinking. Truth was, she was happy to see him. They tore into the fresh catch. I smiled as I watched.

I handed the binoculars to Red. He's lived here most of his life and has seen this spectacle of nature many times, but he never tires of it. He gazed in amazement, like it was the first time. From underneath the glasses he said, "It never gets old, does it? The marvels of nature can unfold right before your very eyes." He pulled the binoculars down and continued talking. "Like dolphins. You know what I mean. We see them almost every day, but we never ignore them. We always stop to watch, even if for a bit."

"Red," I said. "I love it here, dude. Finding this town, this coast, and you folks. It's one of the best things that could have ever happened to me. It isn't only wildlife that finds refuge here."

"Yeah, I know what you mean." Red skipped a beat and then said, "You know. I don't know what heaven is like, or what to expect. But if it's anything less than the Cape, I'm going to be disappointed."

"Me too, brother," I said. "Me too."

I put the boat back into gear to work it toward deeper water and said, "You know. I think I'm ready for that beer. Dig deep down in the ice and get me a cold one. Let's go get a line wet."

The depth of the water behind Pig Island was like the fishing: thin. I wasn't looking or expecting to catch much. I wanted to see the tree line from behind the island. Red had already caught dinner and put his rod away. I kept fishing.

I continued to cast and work the shore toward the island. Red sat on the bow and watched me as he drank beer. He concentrated on each cast. He never said anything. Just sat there watching. I tried to ignore him, but he continued to sit, intently watching my every move. This went on for a dozen casts or so and started to annoy me. Then, in mid-cast, I dropped the rod tip into the water and said, "What? What is it? What are you doing, Red? You're creeping me out, sitting there like that."

"I'm waiting," said Red.

"Waiting on what?"

"Waiting to see if it can really happen."

Frustrated, I asked, "What in the hell are you talking about? Waiting to see if what really happens?"

Red chuckled, "Miracles. I want to see if miracles come true."

"Really? Miracles?"

"Yep!" he laughed and chuckled, saying, "You catch a fish. It'll be a freaking miracle."

Red gave up on witnessing any divine intervention and turned around and sprawled out on the bow of the boat, head over the side to focus on the bottom. We were in about two feet of water, perfect for viewing the blue crab, mullet, stingrays, and other creatures that make up the waters and bay floor. Now and again, Red would reach down and snatch an unsuspecting scallop from the sea floor and make quick work of picking the sweet meat from its shell. They make the perfect snack, much better than the tins of sardines or smoked oysters I kept on board.

Red had a beer sitting next to him. A sweat line made a perfect ring about halfway down the can. Red won't use a Koozie. He claims no need; beers don't stick around long enough to get warm. Either way, the sight made me thirsty.

I made an extra-long cast toward shore and, while the bait was still in the air, I reached down with one hand to open the cooler. At about the same time my bait hit the surface, my hand hit the ice and reached deep past the three trout Red had caught and found me some blue mountains on a can of Coors Light.

With the can in my hand, I used my palm to turn the crank a half turn and closed the bail on my spinning reel. Then I gave the crank a quick, hard turn, allowing the reel to spin freely to take up the slack in the line. The reel spun freely as I lowered the rod tip to reduce the line tension, allowing the bail to recover as much line as possible. At the same time, I was at work bracing the bottom of my beer against my hip to get a nail under the tab.

Opening a fresh, cold beer makes me smile, especially when thirsty. As the tab pulls up and the scored aluminum tears away, the release of carbonation is easy on the ears. Plus, as the compressed gas rushes to the atmosphere, the top of the knuckle almost always gets a cool, refreshing, misty spray, always worthy of a little finger lick.

I was about to take my first swig, when in the distance, I heard the clang of a bell. It rang twice, or so I thought. I stopped to listen. I was quiet. Nothing.

I took my first sip of beer and raised my rod, bringing the bait off the bottom of the bay. The stink bait hadn't taken flight six inches when the line violently went tight. I hadn't even swallowed yet, and I almost bit my tongue. My grip was light, and the fish the rod nearly pulled from my fingers. But I clamped down around the Ugly Stick and instinctively went to set the hook one-handed.

I put my beer down to settle into battle. But by the time I put my hand back on the crank, the line went slack. I raised the rod tip over my head quickly, looking for the fish's presence. I made a couple turns on the reel. Nothing. He was gone. I lowered my rod tip in disappointment, looked to the heavens and screamed, "Son... of... a... Bitch! Dammit!"

From the bow of the boat I heard an unexcited Red say, "You probably won't get any miracles like that. You must have patience. Patience, Grasshopper."

I turned to look at Red and smiled. He hadn't even looked up. He was still gazing at the water over the bow. I was about to give him a ration of shit, not for his Grasshopper wisecrack, but for the crack of his ass. Half of it was on display. The elastic waistband on his swim trunks was worn, and the drawstring untied. It wasn't pretty, but the crack of another man's ass never is.

I was about to say something when the tip of my rod took a quick and powerful turn to the left. My eyes opened like coffee cup saucers. I hadn't lost the fish; he had swum toward the boat and was now making a run down the channel.

"Patience my ass, Red. Fish on!"

It was a great fish and a great fighter. The curve of the rod tip pointed down and out toward the fish's location. It was beautiful. I kept reminding myself not to get too excited. *Easy now. Steady pressure. Let him do the work. Easy now.* I wanted to see it. I wanted it in the boat, but I took my time reeling him in, trying my best to exercise great patience. I kept telling myself. *The fight is half the fun.*

I kept the rod tip high and reeled in quick and easy as I dropped the end of the rod toward the water, never letting the line get too slack. *Steady pressure. Steady pressure.* I slowly brought the rod tip back up to about twelve o'clock, bringing the great fish closer before dropping the tip to reel in again. *Keep it slow and methodical.*

He made another hard run for it, stronger than before. Everything was too tight, including the drag on the reel. I thought the line would break at any moment, my greatest fear. I did not want to lose this fish and he continued to pull, harder and harder. I let go of the crank and quickly made an adjustment to the drag. The reel sang, giving back pressure and line.

And that was how it went for the next ten minutes. I would take in, and he would take back. Luckily, I was on the winning side of the back and forth. After a while, the reel no longer gave back as much of my gains. The fish was getting tired and as it got closer to the boat, I saw it, a big trout.

Red saw it too and said, "Well, son of a bitch. Miracles do happen. I'm a believer now. Great fish, Nigel."

"Tell me about it later. Let's get the damn thing in the boat," I said. "Get the net ready."

Red coached me on. "Easy now. Be careful. He'll make one last run of it once he gets to the boat. You wait and see."

And that's what the fish did. Red had slid the net into the water, and I was trying to guide the fish toward the opening when the big trout made one last stand. The pole bent down and away as the reel's drag sang one last song, taking back what seemed like about 25 feet of line. When he stopped, he was done. I worked him back toward the boat; I could tell he was surrendering.

Red waited with the net and scoop it up. "This is one of the biggest trout I've seen pulled from the bay in a long time. And one of the heaviest for damn sure."

"Be easy with him, now," I said. "He's wore slap-ass out and we still need to get him back in the water. Get the camera."

"Get him back into the water! Have you lost the keys to your mind? What are you talking about?"

In Florida, Spotted Trout have a minimum and maximum size limit. For a trout to qualify for the cooler treatment, it cannot be less than 15 inches or more than 19. There is one exception, though. Each angler can keep one trout over 19 inches. A trophy fish.

"I know, Red. But I'd rather let it go. The memory of landing him and a couple good happy snaps from the camera is all I need. We'll let it go to catch another day."

Red grumbled, chattering to himself as he pulled my camera out of the bag. I picked up the fish and removed the stink bait from his lip. I placed him against the fish rule mounted on the side of the boat; 29 inches, a damn fine fish.

I held him up for the camera as Red took several shots. I enjoyed the moment and knew I would probably never catch another one like that again. My smile was big, but as I held the fish up for the last shot, my smile got even bigger. I was now looking past Red and the camera, focusing beyond. There in the tree line were the two nests, positioned almost as represented in the ransom picture. Then I heard it again, the clang of a bell.

I quickly put the fish back in the water. I gently moved him through the water, forcing water across its gills. The fish began to respond and slowly swam out of my fingers. Before he was free of my hands, he gave his tail a burst of action and shot away, full speed ahead. A great fish. Then, I heard the bell again. It was coming from the island. I looked but saw nothing.

I rinsed and rubbed what remained of the fish off my hands and stood up, drying my hands against my shorts. Red was still bitching about letting the fish go. He was bent over putting my camera away, mumbling to himself, something about a huge disgrace and how it could have fed a small army. I smiled.

"Red, could you do me one more favor after you get through putting the camera away?"

He stood back up, turned toward me, and passed an inquisitive look.

Grinning, I said, "Could you do something with your damn shorts. I've been looking at the top half of your ass for the past hour and that's wrong, man. Just wrong to do a brother that way."

"Oh," Red said. "I didn't realize. Sorry about that. I didn't mean to short-change you."

Then he turned around, bent over, and dropping his trunks to his ankles. All in one swift motion. Chuckling he said, "Here's the other half. The full package."

I squinted and gritted my teeth as I looked away. I shouldn't have said anything. Live and learn.

I was cleaning the fish and the memory of Red's full monty out of my head. I was filleting the last of the trout when my phone bonged. *A text message.* I leaned over to look at the screen. I saw the name: Kim. I put the knife down and grabbed a wad of paper towels, wiped my hands best I could and picked up the phone. The message was only three words: *Where are you?*

It puzzled me at first. Then, it hit me. "Oh shit!" I said. My mind spun. What day was it? What time was it? She was at the airport, Panama City, over two hours away. Crap!

If there's one thing about retirement, it promotes the carefree passage of time. When you live alone, are accountable to nobody but yourself, and void of reasons to think otherwise, every day is a Saturday. The other days–Monday, Tuesday, Wednesday, Yada, Yada, Yada–fade away. For this reason, I live and die by my Google calendar and schedule all important events there. Well, most of them anyway.

Kim Tillman is an old girlfriend. We knew each other from the Navy, and she still serves on active duty. At the time she was a Lieutenant in the Nurse Corp, working at the Naval Hospital in Portsmouth, VA. She was a junior officer; I was senior enlisted, a simple distinction that complicated things from time to time.

Kim outranked me, but we didn't work together. Like many junior officers, she didn't know shit about the Navy. Commanding Officers rely on their chiefs to covertly train junior officers, so they don't... well... quite frankly... fuck up in front of the other sailors. If an officer does something too stupid, too early in their career, the time it takes to earn back the respect of the crew can be long and painful. Some never recover and remain ineffective for the rest of their time in service. Word travels fast in the Navy.

Lieutenants are not too bad. By the time they make O3, they have been around a few years. They don't need the same handholding as ensigns and lieutenant junior grades. The more junior officers have an innate ability to take a simple task and turn it into a complete soup sandwich. As a chief, it was one of my jobs to prevent that, to turn fresh, wet-behind-the-ear officers into sailors.

With Kim, if we could separate the Navy from our personal lives, we were good together. That wasn't always easy, and Kim was better at keeping the two worlds apart. She could leave work and the Navy at the door, but she was a nurse in a hospital. I was a sailor on a ship, a huge difference. I didn't have a door to leave anything behind. Even off duty, I lived and breathed the Navy. By choice, I lived the life twenty-four hours a day, seven days a week. I slept on the ship or my sailboat at the base marina and ate most of my meals aboard. I lounged away, night after night, in the chief's mess. I was constantly surrounded by the world's most powerful Navy. I was comfortable there. It was home.

Lieutenant Tillman and I had been seeing each other for about ten months. Occasionally when the paths of our personal and professional lives crossed, we handled it without incident. We would both take a step back and collect our common sense. Unfortunately, events leading up to our last date didn't work out so smoothly.

We had plans, important plans for a nice dinner and a play, *Phantom of the Opera*. I'm not one for theater and such, but I knew it was one of her favorites. When I saw it was coming to town, I surprised her with tickets, opening night, second row. I made the reservations and bought the theater tickets several weeks in advance. We were both looking forward to the night. Then, late in the afternoon, on the day of the show, there was a change of plans.

Kevin Barry was one of my junior chiefs. His anchors had been pinned on only two months prior. I was his sponsor during his initiation and honored when he asked me to pin on his starboard anchor on his big day. His young wife, Karen, some six months pregnant, pinned on the port side.

During the pinning ceremony, three others were celebrating their promotion that day. Kevin was the last to be pinned. Karen and I made our way to the front of the room where he waited. He was standing tall and proud. Unless you have experienced it, you wouldn't understand. Earning your anchors is one of the finest days in the life of any sailor. It defines, with an exclamation point, one's enlisted career, a transformation from a strong, two-tone blue first class petty officer, to a world of senior enlisted. It's the proudest and most emotional day in the life of a sailor.

As we approach him, he was stone-faced, full of pride. We stopped in front of him and I turned to his wife and said, "He looks good. Wouldn't you say, Karen?"

"Absolutely, Nigel. Absolutely."

"There seems to be something missing, though."

"Yes, he looks pretty naked there. Maybe we should do something about that."

"I agree."

I walked up and whispered in Kevin's ear, "You know, when this is all over, you'll be able to call me Nigel too. Like your lovely bride."

He said nothing. He stood there at attention displaying superb control and discipline. Karen and I ceremoniously pinned the anchors on his collars, and then we stood back. "That's better," I said.

It was a proud moment for me too. I had watched and guided this young man for the past four years. He was a fine quartermaster and an outstanding leader who had made my life easier. He had been operating as a chief for over a year. This made it official, and my heart felt warm by the sight of him. Then I thought, as his sponsor and mentor, he probably needed one last lesson in humility.

I took a little step forward and very quietly asked, "Chief Barry. Are you going to cry?"

His eyes were strong, set forward and ahead. He said nothing.

"I asked you a question, Chief. I recommend you look at me and answer."

He turned his eyes toward me and tried his best to maintain composure. When he saw my quivering smile and a small, single tear stream down my starboard cheek, it was all over. It was more than he could bear. The flood gates opened. Years of study, preparation and sacrifice, coupled with weeks of tough initiation flowed from him. It was the great relief he needed. It was all over. He was now Chief Barry, his life forever transformed. It would never be the same, all for the better.

I was getting ready for my date with Kim. I had showered and was finishing up shaving when the door to the head flew open and I heard my name being called with great excitement. "Nigel! Nigel!"

"Over here, dammit. Over here. What's the fuss?"

It was Kevin. He was bent over, hand on his knees and out of breath, trying to talk. "It's here, Nigel. It's here." He took a couple of deeper breaths before continuing. "Well... not here yet, not exactly anyway, but coming. That's for sure. It's on its way."

I said, "For Christ's sake, Kevin. What the hell are you talking about?"

"It's Karen, Nigel. Karen."

"Karen. Okay. Good. She's on her way over. Great..."

"No, goddammit! Not Karen. The baby. The baby is coming."

"The baby! Holy shit!" I said. "Wait... the baby isn't due for another three or four weeks, right?"

"I guess nobody told the little fella. He's on his own program."

"Outstanding. Where is Karen now?"

"She's in an ambulance. On her way to the hospital, Portsmouth Naval."

"Then why in the hell are you talking to me? Get your ass out of here. With Hampton Boulevard traffic, it's going to take you forever to get there. You're wasting time, knucklehead. Get the hell out of here."

"Nigel. I'm on duty. I can't leave."

He was right. Under normal circumstances he would have to remain on board the rest of the day and throughout the night. These weren't normal circumstances, though. The decision was a no brainer.

"Bullshit," I said. "Get your skinny ass out of here. I'll cover your duty."

"But Chief, I can't ask you to do that. Plus, you have your big date tonight. What about Kim? I can't..."

I interrupted, "You haven't asked me to do anything. I'm telling you, and, if I must kick your ass, it will only waste more time. Karen needs you. Now get your ass off this ship. Pronto! I'll square everything away with the CDO."

"But Chief, the CDO is Mr. Stiles."

"I know who is on duty. You let me take care of Mr. Stiles. Now go, dammit! Go, before you piss me off!"

He turned and ran out the door.

I stood there in front of the mirror, remnants of shaving cream still on my face. I reached down, turned on the cold water, wet my washcloth, and placed it over my face. I held it there until the chill of the water was gone. I pulled it down, around my face and ears, then I looked at myself in the mirror. How was I going to break the news to Kim? Before that, I had to deal with the CDO.

I walked back into berthing and put on a fresh set of khakis, nicely pressed. I squared away my gig line then went to the wardroom to find Mr. Stiles, the command duty officer for the day.

Commander Stiles was new on board, a Supply Corps officer from an AO, an auxiliary oiler ship. I didn't particularly like him, but neither did anyone else. I didn't care for the way he treated both his junior officers and enlisted men alike. He was an ass, an unhappy guy. He'd been passed over for the rank of captain three times which meant his days in the Navy were numbered. Three tries and you're out. *If he couldn't be happy, no one else could be either.* That was how he planned to carry out his remaining time in the Navy.

When I entered the wardroom, he was sitting at the dining room table, paperwork spread out in front of him.

"Evening, sir," I said.

"I'm busy, Chief Logan. Later."

"That's fine, sir. This won't take long."

He tried to ignore me, his face peering down into mounds of paperwork, probably orders and requisitions of some logistical nightmare. Perhaps it was tons of spoiled cabbage and bananas, or maybe he was trying to figure out how much rice to buy for the traditional Friday fish selection. Who knows? I didn't care.

"I wanted to let you know, sir. I've taken over the duty for Chief Barry. He has a family emergency. He had to go. So, I sent him on his way."

He looked up. "He's already left the ship. He's gone ashore?"

"Yes, sir."

"Who approved that?"

"I did, sir."

"Who in the hell do you think you are? I'm the CDO. I'm the only one that can authorize that. You're way the fuck out of line here, Chief. Call his ass and tell him to get back to the ship, immediately."

I looked around the room. There were three other junior officers in the room. I gave them a look, a hidden message. They took the hint and got up to leave us alone, in private. Stiles stopped them. "All of you sit back down. I may need witnesses."

"Sir, no disrespect intended," I said. "I would have cleared this with you earlier. There simply wasn't time. It's his wife. She's having a baby, three weeks early. It's their first. There wasn't time."

"I don't give a shit about that, Chief. I missed the birth of my first child, sitting in the middle of the Indian Ocean, resupplying a battle group, supporting the war effort. So, don't give me any of that weak-ass bullshit. I won't hear it. Now get him on the phone. I want him standing in this wardroom, at attention, within the hour. Get on it!"

I looked around and took a quick glance at the other officers in the room: two lieutenants and one butter-bar ensign. They were looking at their laps, embarrassed of what they were forced to watch. I turned back toward Stiles and gave him a cold look, no expression. Then I walked over to the phone, picked it up and dialed Kevin's cell phone number. It rang twice before he picked up.

"Chief Barry. Chief Logan here."

I looked back across the room at Commander Stiles. We maintained eye contact for the entire conversation. I wanted to see his face. "Where are you? Have you made it to the hospital yet?" I listened, as the CDO and I continued our glare. Kevin was almost to the mid-town tunnel. "That's fine," I said. "Listen, Chief. I need you to do something for me. I'm really sorry, but I need you to stop and turn around."

I watched as Stiles grinned, feeling ever confident in battle. He was in control and loving every second. Power is a wonderful thing. Its abuse is another. Then I watched, with great satisfaction, as I pulled the spoils of victory right out from underneath him.

"Yeah, that's right, turn around. There is a florist back on the corner of Hampton and Fantail. I have an account there. Talk to Lisa. I want you to go back and pick up a big bundle of flowers. Tell Karen they're from me and the rest of the department. Put them on my account and don't go cheap on me. And one last thing. After you kiss her for yourself, give her one for me. You got that?"

I listened as Kevin thanked me. Then I said, "Well, get going, shipmate. We've already wasted enough time here."

I hung up the phone without looking down, my eyes still peering into the now rage-laden pupils of Stiles. I turned toward the other officers. They were no longer looking down. The two lieutenants had small, simple smiles; the ensign was in shock, shaking in fear, scared to death. What a pussy. He needs work.

Stiles slammed his fist down onto the table. "Goddamn you!"

"Sir, I'm sorry. Your duty section is intact. The officer of the deck has been notified. I have the watch. Everything is in good hands. If you need me, I'll be in my office."

I turned and walked to the door. Stiles was furious, out of control with anger. He pounded his fist on the table again and again. "Chief! You haven't heard the end of this, you insubordinate son of a bitch!"

"I figure you're right, sir." I thought for a moment and said, "No hard feelings, sir. You have to do, what you have to do, and I have to do what chiefs do. It all works out in the end. Trust me. Good evening, sir."

Then, I opened the door and walked out. Halfway down the passage-way I realized I had to go back. I couldn't help myself.

I stepped back into the wardroom. "Sorry to interrupt again, sir. But I was thinking you may want to go ahead and give the skipper a call. Call him at home, sir. I'm sure he'd want to know about this."

"You are excused, Chief. Get the hell out of this wardroom! I will speak to the old man in the morning. I won't disturb his evening over some rogue, inconsiderate, and disrespectful CPO. I will leave him to his peace."

"This? You mean, tonight? Our little disagreement? Well... no, not at all, sir. I wouldn't bother him with that at all. But you might want to inform him that Chief Barry's wife is about to have a baby. He will probably want to send flowers too. He may want you to go ahead and arrange to have something sent. You know, from himself and the crew. We both use the same florist. Would you like the number?"

"Get out of my wardroom! Now! Go! Before I call the Master at Arms."

"As you wish, sir. Thank you." I turned and exited; a smile cracked across my face as soon as the door slammed. *What an Asshole.*

I went to my office and sat at my desk. It was exhausting dealing with Commander Stiles. "He's such a dick," I said aloud. Then I thought of a classic line from a Robin Williams movie, *Good Morning Vietnam*. The young Adrian Cronauer, played by Williams, was being dressed down by Sergeant Major Dickerson while he was being involuntarily discharged from service. As Cronauer left the office, he stopped at the door to say, "You know? You're in more dire need of a blow job than any white man in history." I smiled and laughed.

The skipper would have mixed emotions about what transpired between Stiles and me. I knew that. If there was one person who dislikes Stiles more than I do, it's the skipper. He hated the guy too. As a proper course of good order and discipline, that isn't something he would share with anyone except maybe his executive officer and even that was unlikely.

Captain Charles Matthews is the consummate naval professional, an exceptional officer and even better commanding officer. He is fair and very good to his crew. In exchange, he holds those that serve underneath him to the highest standards. He expects nothing short of excellence.

Rarely does the crew let him down. I did and felt bad about it. I like him, always have.

It wasn't planned, but the captain and I have served together under two other commands. They reassigned me to the USS Davenport, a Perry Class Frigate out of Mayport, FL the year I made chief. He was finishing up his last few months as the ship's First Lieutenant. He was over the deck department. I didn't work for him, but we worked together until he departed for his next duty station.

Several years later our paths crossed again. We found ourselves in Naples, Italy. We had shore duty with the Sixth Fleet Command, on the Naval Support Activity, Capodichino. Over the years we grew to admire and respect each other. We formed a friendship built on trust, a trust that allowed him to use me as a sounding board whenever he needed to vent, always in the strictness of confidence. We became close friends off duty, but always sailors when it counted.

Over beers or whiskey, we had more than one conversation about Commander Stiles, so I knew how he felt. But that wouldn't take away from the fact that I had disrespected and embarrassed Stiles, especially in front of other junior officers. As good as the moment felt, I would have to own up and make it right for Charley. That won't be a problem, anything for the old man. I would call him later to give him a heads-up and to apologize.

Before I did anything else, I had to call Kim, break the news to her, and ruin what would have been a perfect evening. I looked at the phone, took a deep breath, and picked it up.

She took the news worse than I thought. Her disappointment was expected. Hell, I was disappointed too, but I wasn't expecting real anger. I thought I could rely on her sense of duty, her understanding of the Navy, and how sometimes things don't always work out the way you plan.

I could have applied that logic to Chief Barry. *Sorry shipmate. That just sucks. Too bad you're going to miss it. Your wife will be fine. Welcome to the Navy. Enjoy your duty. I got to go.*

That wouldn't have been right, though. Missing the birth of his first child would carry far more disappointment than my missing some stupid play. And besides, if they decide to have more children, chances are very high he won't be around when they are born. The life of a quartermaster is spent at sea.

"Change of plans? You have got to be kidding me, right?" she said. "I mean, you're serious? We're not going?"

"I'm so sorry, Kim. You can take a girlfriend. Go without me. It's one of those unavoidable things," I said.

"It is one of those bullshit things. That's what it is. And what do you mean by unavoidable? That's horseshit. He knew we had plans. He could have asked someone else to stand in for him. Hell, you could have pulled someone else, so don't give me that unavoidable shit."

"Kim. Dammit. I said I was sorry. And he didn't ask me to do anything, and I didn't have anyone else to impose on, not that I would have, anyway."

"You mean you, you volunteered?"

"Yes, I did, but…"

"Really! You volunteered! Well, isn't that wonderful?"

I didn't say a thing. I got quiet while she carried on, bitching about one thing or another. She was revealing a side that I hadn't yet seen, a side I didn't like.

She couldn't look past her wants and needs. She wasn't even willing to consider the position I was in. I was disappointed too, but the needs of our people far outweigh either of our wants. Things were going downhill and instead of an argument with her boyfriend, Chief Logan surfaced to deal with a spoiled, out-of-line junior officer.

"That's enough. You can stand down, LT, and listen. Obviously, you haven't learned the value of taking care of your people. You've never put anyone above yourself. You wear a Navy uniform, but you have no idea the sacrifices others make when it's worn. But, how would you? You're a nurse, in a safe, little hospital. You work your nine-to-five each day and go home, like a regular job. You get to play Navy but are clueless to the real work of the fleet and what the Navy does. That's the difference between you and me. You're in the Navy and I'm a sailor. Unlike you, I know the sacrifices my men make. I ask a lot of them, so, when their backs are against the wall, I'm obligated to step in. Do you get that?

I'm obligated. And that obligation runs far deeper than any night on the town, regardless of the circumstances. It always will. Are we clear on that?"

It got quiet on the phone. There was only static from the terrible ship-to-shore phone connection.

Kim, finally said, "Nigel, I..."

Frustrated, I interrupted but spoke in a more understanding tone. I only wanted to get off the line before I made matters worse. "Listen. Grab a girlfriend. Go to the play. The tickets are under my name at the theater. I'll call to let them know you'll be picking them up. Enjoy yourself. Perhaps one day you'll understand, but right now I got to go. I need to prepare for the eight o'clock reports. I'll talk to you later." Then I hung up the phone. *Dammit!*

We wouldn't talk again for months.

Before I retired and left town, Kim and I tried to reconcile. She wanted to work out our issues and regain what we once had. I was receptive, but skeptical. *How could things be the same?* We were enjoying modest success when my life was turned upside down, thrown in a spin. I was consumed with legal problems that left no time for a personal life, certainly not a relationship. That was the last thing I needed or wanted. When I retired, I disappeared and left without saying goodbye.

Looking down at my fish cleaning station, I tried to remember the details. Kim had called a few weeks ago. I was reluctant to answer, but I did. It was the first contact with my prior life since arriving in Port St. Joe. We spoke on the phone for about an hour, and I was thankful she didn't bring up the past. We talked about this and that, her promotion to lieutenant commander, and everything else that was going on in her life. Then she invited herself for a visit, to spend a few days so we could talk and spend time together. She caught me in a weak moment, and I agreed.

She was to fly in late afternoon on a Monday, which was today and leave the following Thursday. *Crap! Why didn't I put it on the calendar?*

I worked fast to finish up the last trout, butchering up the filet. I left more meat on the bone than I put in the freezer bag. That pissed me off. *Stupid me*. I ran inside the house and washed my hands, then called her. She picked up on the first ring.

"Kim. I'm sorry. I had something come up. I'm nowhere near the airport. Still at the house and about to leave."

"Did you forget I was coming?"

"No, not at all," I lied. "It's crazy around here. Sit tight. It will take a while to get there, but I'm on my way."

After a three-minute Navy shower, I threw on some clothes. Five minutes later, a little past 1830, I was on the road, racing down Highway 98 toward Panama City. The tourist traffic in Mexico Beach slowed me down. With no place to pass, all I could do was grin and bear it. *Why didn't I put it on the calendar, dammit?*

When I crossed the bridge on the other side of Mexico Beach things opened, I pressed hard. Her words came back to me. *Did you forget I was coming?* More than that, it was the lie I told that kept ringing in my ear, haunting me. No, not at all. No, not at all. That bothered me more. Then my phone bonged again. *What now?*

This time it was an email, a Google calendar alert. I read the screen: *Remember! Poker tonight with Joe Crow and the boys, 1930.*

I drove on for a few minutes, listening to what was ping-ponging in my head. *Did you forget I was coming? No, not at all. No, not at all. Did you forget I was coming?* "Dammit," I said. Then I looked again at the new email reminder on the phone.

Joe Crow and his wife Ruby have a place out on the Cape. One of the best lots, ever. It's on the bay side, on the cut behind Pig Island. It's the best of two worlds, beautiful and well protected from both the weather of the gulf and the bay. It's peaceful, quiet, and hosts a million-dollar view.

Joe is a retired tugboat captain from Mobile, Alabama. A spirited, colorful sort, as most people are that have made their living at sea. He wasn't your typical tug operator, servicing cargo ships entering port and making berth at a terminal. He was a seagoing tug captain, pulling or pushing loaded barges all over the Gulf of Mexico and the Caribbean.

We met one evening while I was warming stool seventeen at the Reid Avenue Bar and Package, *The City Bar* as Joe likes to call it. Candice, the full-time bartender, introduced us and kept our glasses full. We were two sailors in a bar. It didn't take long before we hit it off. For hours we swapped lies and yarns. A few stories may have contained a thread or two of truth, but sailors know the difference. Either way, Joe was a new friend.

Joe likes to play cards. He and several other locals get together about once a week for poker night. He's been after me to join them for months: guy time, poker, food, and beer. It sounded like fun. I wanted to go, but it seemed I always had something going on. But, one night last week, while picking crabs at their place, he brought it up again. His wife Ruby put her hands down on the table and said, "Nigel! Please! Would you please go? If you do, then maybe he'll shut up about it."

I laughed and pulled out my phone to look at my schedule. It was an open date, or at least I thought it was, so I committed. "Absolutely!" I said. "Wouldn't miss it for the world." It was the truth.

Eyes focused straight ahead; I was running wide open to Panama City and frustrated. Now I had another voice in my head. *Absolutely. Wouldn't miss it for the world. Wouldn't miss it for the world.* I found myself caught between a truth and a lie. I slammed my fist on the steering wheel. *Son of a bitch!*

The truck started to slow. I wasn't thinking and had taken my foot off the gas pedal. I damn near stopped in the middle of the road. A car passed me fast. Its horn blaring the whole time brought me around. *Damn, Logan. Get off the highway before you kill somebody.* I pulled over to the side of the road.

What a day. It had been a long one, and I was tired. I picked up the phone and made a call.

She answered on the first ring. "Kim," I said. "I'm sorry. The truth is... I'm not coming to get you."

She didn't like what I had to say and who could blame her. The truth was I had forgotten she was coming. I had no excuse. I guess I didn't want to see her. I wasn't ready to dig up the past and no short visit was going to change that, not now, net ever. I apologized and told her it would be best if she went back home. I told her to stay a few days in Panama City if she liked, but we wouldn't be seeing each other. I apologized one last time.

She lambasted me with colorful metaphors, calling me every name in the book. I let her have her say as she went on and on. There was no argument from me. I didn't have one, and long before she hung up the phone, I was already headed back to Port St. Joe. I had a poker game to go to.

It was midmorning when I pulled into the filling station to top off my pickup truck. The automatic nozzle clicked off at $46.37, but I squeezed in some more, rounding it off to $48.00. I like stopping at a full dollar amount. At the counter, I reached into my pocket. *Oh Crap!* I pulled the pockets of my shorts inside out; piles of lint fell to the floor. *Damn!* Then I remembered.

My night of poker with Joe Crow and company went well as I expected: a wash. They cleaned me out. My fifty dollar buy-in dwindled after the very first hand. I never recovered. I won a few hands, but I couldn't build a single dollar of surplus. However, what I lost financially was more than made up for by good times, good laughs, and good food with new friends. I'll do it again, if invited back. And I'm guessing, if I'm willing to show up and leave my fifty bucks somewhere around the room, I'll always have a seat at the table.

I'm not much of a player, never have been. On my last ship, my fellow chiefs played all the time. I never paid them much mind, never really had much of an interest. It wasn't my thing. So, on this first night at the table, neither lady nor beginner's luck shone on me. I heard the words of Kim

Tillman echo in my head. *You're a loser, Nigel Logan. Nothing but a loser.* I laughed at myself.

I looked up and smiled at the clerk. He asked, "A little short?"

"Yeah. Looks that way."

"That's okay. Come back and pay me later."

"That would be great, Timmy," I said reading the name off his name tag. "I appreciate it. I'll be back a little later after I make a run to the bank."

As I left, I got to thinking. What just happened was one of the great things about this town and area. There is a level of trust and honesty about those that live here. Strangers get caught off guard by the unexpected kindness.

There are few places left in the world where you'd be able to drive away owing any merchant any sum of money at all. Timmy isn't even the owner of the store. He's a clerk, and a damn good one too. Not worried a lick, he knows I'll be back.

My bank isn't a financial institution, but a lockbox where I keep a large stash of money, enough to sustain me. I withdrew all but a couple hundred dollars out of my Navy Federal Credit Union accounts before I left Tidewater. My naval pension goes into one of those accounts, but I haven't withdrawn the first dollar since leaving. I could have used my debit or credit card, but I didn't want to. Others back in Norfolk would be keeping an eye on those accounts, so I pay cash for everything. I don't want to leave an electronic footprint of my whereabouts. If they want to find me that bad, they could do it the hard way.

Back at the house, I walked in and closed all the blinds for privacy. The old house I rent was originally built with a small fireplace. For some reason, it had been closed off with tongue-and-groove wood paneling to match the rest of the room, but it is anything but seamless. With the television moved away from the wall, there's no hiding the patchwork. The chimney on the roof is another hint that the place had once been heated by fire.

I worked the makeshift panel from the wall and took out my lockbox. I punched in my security code and opened it. I looked inside and grinned. Seeing those wrapped bundles of $100.00 bills would make anybody smile, each weighing in at ten thousand dollars. There are sixteen full bundles and a partial, almost one hundred seventy thousand dollars. They represent the fruits of a frugal life in the navy. I slipped a couple bills out of the partial bundle and put everything back as I found it. *Perfect.*

I strolled back into the filling station. Timmy was behind the counter reading an old Spiderman comic book, or graphic novel as they are known these days. He was wearing white gloves and handling the thing as if it were one of the original copies of the Declaration of Independence. Turns out, to him, it practically was. He's a collector.

"What you got there, Timmy?"

He looked up, carefully closed it and gently put it down on a piece of black felt. "It's a classic. A 1963 Spiderman comic. It's from the first series, *Death Without Warning*. I got it yesterday. I won it off an online auction. I was looking over its condition before putting it back into its case."

"How much did that set you back?" I asked.

"I try not to think about it, so I'd rather not say. It's worth every penny though. I actually got a good deal on it."

He picked it back up to show me. It looked to be in excellent condition. I saw the original cover price in the corner.

"I'm going to guess you paid a bit more than fifteen cents?"

"Yes, Sir," he said smiling. "That much I will let on. A little bit more than that."

He told me he had over one thousand comics, about two hundred fifty were of collector's quality. The others would have to cook for a few years before there would be a market for them in the community. *The Community*, the comic book underground that covets such items.

Some folks invest in stocks and bonds, others in gold and silver. Timmy puts his money in comic books. He's probably a lot smarter than most people give him credit for.

My phone bonged. A text message. It was from Candice. It had only two words: *call me.*

I paid Timmy for my gas and tossed him an additional five-dollar bill. It wasn't much, but he appreciated it. He tried not to take it at first, but I insisted. I told him to put it toward his next comic auction. He smiled.

I called Candice from the truck.

"Nigel," she said. "You need to get over here. I'm at work. There is something I need to show you."

"Kind of early to be offering libations, wouldn't you say?" I asked.

"I'm not open. Just came in to get ahead of some paperwork. Please get over here."

"What's wrong, Candice?"

"It's Luke, Nigel. Get over here."

I was only a couple blocks away, so I got there in no time.

Except for Candice's pink Jeep Wrangler, the stretch of Reid Avenue in front of the bar was empty. I parked right in front of the door. I hadn't even put the truck into park when I saw it. It had to be what Candice called about.

It was a poster taped to the front window right next to the door. I shook my head, got out of the truck, and walked up to the poster to get a better look. It had a big picture of Maxine on the front with the words, *WANTED DEAD or ALIVE... $100.00 to the man or woman that brings me the vermin that kidnapped my precious Maxine.* Underneath that, Luke left his name and cell phone number.

Candice opened the door. Her new hair color was a medium brown, sort of hazelnut with blond highlights. She looked good. It was much better than the almost pumpkin orange she sported the week before.

"Hey, Sweetheart," she said. "That didn't take long. Admit it. You missed me, didn't you?"

"Come on now, Candice. Knock it off and throw me a bone here. What's this all about?"

Hands on her waist, hips cocked off to one side, she said, "Throw you a bone? How about you throw me one?"

"Candice!"

She threw her hands up in the air and turned around. "Oh! You're no fun. Come inside."

I ripped the poster off the window, wadded it up and went through the door. At the bar Candice said, "Yesterday, about an hour or so after you left, Luke got up and hurried to the door. I asked him where he was going and he said, 'To get Maxine back. The old school way. Nigel was right.

This has to be handled internally.' Then he flew out the door. What did he mean by that, Nigel?"

My words came back to me. *This probably needs to be handled internally, without the authorities. Sometimes the legalities of things get in the way.* "Oh, shit!" I said. "It was something I said. Something I told him yesterday, here at the bar. But this isn't what I had in mind. Did you see him this morning?"

"No. But I'm guessing he has a pretty big stack of posters. I've already seen others about town. I guess he's going all around putting them up wherever he can."

"Crap! I got to go," I said. "I need to find Luke. Will you do me a favor? Ride around. See if you can find any other posters. Take them down. Get rid of them for me. And if you see him before I do, tell him to knock it off and call me."

"I will, if you promise to have dinner with me one night," she said.

"Candice, we don't have time for this kind of thing. We need to help Luke keep from embarrassing himself any more than he already has."

"Come on now, Nigel. One little dinner wouldn't hurt anything. Promise me and I'm all yours."

"Candice..."

"Promise, me."

"Okay... Okay. I promise but get going. We have a lot of ground to cover."

She cut me a wink and said, "Yes. Yes, we do."

Ever since my first night in town, Candice has been trying to secure a date night. I like her fine and she's quite attractive. I'm not sure how an evening together would pan out. She is assertive and outspoken, and I'm not that interested. I'm not much interested in anybody to be honest. But what the hell, a little dinner doesn't have to be anything more than that. She's right; a little dinner wouldn't hurt anything. Besides, I guess I owe her. Not for helping me find Luke and his posters, but for keeping my ass out of jail. On my first night in town, I got a little drunk—okay, a lot drunk—and beat up one of her ex-husbands. It wasn't pretty. My head still hurts thinking about that night.

I pulled out of my parking spot and continued down Reid toward First Street. It didn't take long before I threw on the brakes. There was another poster in the window of Chico's Taqueria. I checked my rearview mirror for oncoming traffic. I threw the truck in park, got out and ran to the window and tore it down. A waiter from inside watched me. My Spanish isn't that good, but I read his lips. *Gracias Senor*.

I turned right on First Street, then an immediate right on Williams. I picked up my phone and tried to call Luke. He didn't pick up. *Damn.* I cruised slow, keeping an eye out. I removed another poster from the hardware store window, another from Gloria's Beauty Shop, and another that was taped over a speed limit sign. *Damn, Luke.*

I rolled on and stopped in the middle of the road. I looked to my right to find another. I backed up then pulled forward into a parking spot. There was a poster taped to another shop window. But it really wasn't a shop anymore. It had been converted to an education center. I sat in my truck and ignored the poster for a bit, to watch the goings-on of the establishment.

Through the window I saw the profile of several desks, six or seven of them filled with individuals of all ages and walks of life. They looked less than interested in the material in front of them. In front of the room facing the students was another much larger desk. Sitting behind it was a prominent pillar of society, a cornerstone of living well. He didn't see me watching at first, but when he reached down into his left desk drawer and quietly recharged his coffee cup with a long pour of Jim Beam, his eyes wandered out the window to find me smiling from behind the windshield. My buddy Red was skillfully preparing another class of students to graduate from RIDD, Red's Institute for Drunk Drivers. He grinned back and held up a finger. *Hold on, I'll be out in a second.*

I met him on the sidewalk outside the door. He had his coffee cup in hand.

"A little early for that, is it not?" I said, nodding toward the cup.

"What?" Red replied in exasperation holding up the cup. "This? Don't be ridiculous. Historically, an early morning bump and daylight indulging was always acceptable. It wasn't until the damn temperance movement that nosey prudes like Susan B. Anthony and crazies like Carrie Nation decided to make such a big deal about it."

"I thought Susan B. Anthony was more noted for her work with the suffrage movement, getting women the right to vote," I said.

"That's true, and she did great work in that arena. But it was her unsuccessful attempts in the temperance movement that drove her to embrace suffrage. They collected over 28,000 signatures in a petition demanding the limitation of liquor sales in the State of New York. The legislature rejected and dismissed it because most of the signatures were from women and children, voices that had no political impact. It was then she realized that if women were going to make an impact on national issues, they needed the right to vote. She shifted gears to concentrate on suffrage."

"You mentioned Carrie Nation," I said. "Who the hell was that?"

"She was a real crazy bitch from Kansas, the original wicked witch of the mid-west. She used to storm into bars and saloons with a hatchet and raise hell at all the men. She would attack the whiskey, busting up bottles of booze. What a pain in the ass. I would never hit a woman, but with Carrie Nation, she was just ugly enough that... who knows what I would have done."

"Where do you get all this shit?" I asked. "How do you know all this stuff?"

"I run a DUI school, Nigel. I must be an authority on the historical aspects of spirits. Plus, I do a lot of reading when I haven't been drinking."

"When the hell is that?" I asked.

With a serious, shit-you-not look on his face, he said, "I'm a quick reader."

I looked at the ground and laughed. There is never a dull moment dealing with Red. He's so damn smart, and he never takes himself too seriously. A quality we should all strive to achieve.

Still laughing, I said, "Listen, I dropped by because of this." I pointed to Luke's poster. "It's wrong and needs to come down."

"I know," said Red. "It's terrible, an awful picture of Maxine."

"No, Red. The whole thing is wrong. It's a bad idea getting worse with each one that goes up. I'm running around trying to find him. I'm afraid he's putting them up faster than I can tear them down. Did you see him this morning? Were you here when he came by?"

"Sure," he said. "I was here. He told me about Maxine. You know that goat isn't my favorite. On more than one occasion I've caught the damn thing drinking my beer. The little shit." Then Red thought for a moment and said, "But I know how much she means to the old coot, so I guess I understand where he's coming from. He told me you were helping him out. That's mighty nice of you."

"Yeah, well it doesn't help when he's out pulling stupid shit like this. Did he say where he was going? What direction he might be headed?"

"Nope. Just that he had a lot of posters and a lot of tape."

"Well that's great," I said. "I have to run. Do me a favor and take that down. And if you come across any others, take them down too."

As I was climbing back into my truck, Red said, "Not a problem. And by the way, are you coming to the raw bar tonight? If so, I'll bring that little something-something I have for you. What I forgot yesterday."

Standing on the running board and looking over the open door, I said, "That's fine. I'll be out there at some point. See ya then."

I rolled up and down the rest of the streets of Port St. Joe, stopping on occasion to tear down more posters. I pulled into the library parking lot on Highway 71 and stopped to think about where Luke might be. I tried to call his cell phone again: no answer.

He could have gone in any of three directions, north up Highway 71 toward Wewa, west out Highway 98 toward Mexico Beach, or flip it east back toward Apalachicola. I headed up Highway 71. If he went toward Wewa, he would most likely stop in White City, just on the other side of the Inner Coastal Waterway and place a poster in the window of the general store. If I find a poster, I'd be on his trail. If not, I could be confident that he hadn't gone that way.

I rolled onto the gravel parking lot of the small filling station and general store. There was no poster in the window. I got out and checked with the folks inside. They all know Luke. *Everybody does.* But they hadn't seen him all morning. I considered that good luck and could eliminate the long drive toward Wewa.

As my truck crossed the railroad tracks coming back into town, my phone rang. I look at the phone. It was Luke McKenzie. I pressed talk.

"Luke McKenzie. Where in the hell are you?" A little aggravation showing through my tone. "I've been looking for you all morning."

"I'm calling you back, you grouchy bastard. I saw where I missed a couple of your calls."

I was quiet for a bit and apologized. "I'm sorry, Luke. It's been a long morning. Where are you?"

"St. Joe Beach, if you have to know. I'm out putting up posters."

"Yeah, I've seen them," I said. "Listen, we need to talk about this approach you've come up with. I don't think it is such a good idea. I recommend taking them all down before somebody else gets the wrong idea."

"The wrong idea? What in hell are you talking about? I think it's pretty clear."

I listened to Luke explain all the reasons it was a good idea. He went on and on. Then he mentioned putting one up in the window of the post office. He was proud of that idea since most wanted posters can be found there. Suddenly, I didn't feel so smart. I should have thought about that as an obvious location already.

Luckily, the post office is off Highway 71, so I was close. I did a quick turn around and whipped into the parking lot. I pulled into a spot directly in front of the poster, right next to a squad car. I sat and watched as two of Port St. Joe's finest examined the poster. After writing notes on a pad, they took a picture of the poster before taking it down. *Shit!*

"Yeah, I know. It was pretty clever," I said rolling my eyes. "But it's not the approach I think we should be taking. Just do me a favor. Don't put up any more posters and meet me at your house. We need to talk. Okay?"

"Do you have some news?" Luke asked.

"I'll tell you everything I know when I see you. Just promise me, no more posters."

"Okay," Luke conceded. "I'll be at the house around noon. Meet me then."

I looked inside Luke's truck as I walked up his drive. The passenger seat had a good stack of posters scattered about. Perhaps that was a good sign. Maybe he hadn't put too many up. I knocked hard on the door then walked over to take a seat on the front porch swing. It was too nice to be inside.

"Come on in!"

"I'm out on the porch, Luke. On the swing, you come on out!"

"Beers!" The entire street had to hear that.

"That would be great. Thanks!"

He came outside with a couple Bud Lights. He looked stressed, tired, and undernourished. He probably hadn't eaten much since the ordeal began. He popped the tops and took a seat on an old metal glider. It must be at least forty years old, a classic. It squeaked something awful when it moved and made one hell of a racket.

"You know, a little oil on the hinges would take care of that," I said.

"Huh?"

"A little oil, maybe some grease. You know, to..." I could tell by the look on his face he was oblivious to what I was referring to. "Forget it."

He said nothing.

"So, have you heard anything?" I asked. "They said they would contact you."

"No, dammit. That's what has me worried. I haven't heard a thing."

"That could be good," I said.

"Or it could be bad. That's why I made the posters. I wanted to step up the game. Like we talked about, you know. Keep it all internal like. Handle it ourselves."

"Luke, listen. That poster thing was a bad idea and by doing so you took it outside. You opened it up to the public. Not good."

He sat there looking ahead, said nothing.

"You can probably expect a call from the Port St. Joe PD. I know they have seen the poster. I watched them take the one down at the post office."

Luke raised his voice out of irritation. "Those bastards. They have no right. They already told me they wouldn't help, that they didn't have time to look for her. And why do they give a shit, anyway?"

"I don't know, Luke. Maybe because your poster incites violence. That's frowned upon in the world of law enforcement."

"To hell with them," he shouted. "I would gladly kill the bastards that did this."

I looked around the street to see if anyone was around. "Dammit, Luke. Would you please hold your voice down? It's not smart to broadcast such things, even if it is a joke."

"But it's not a joke, dammit."

"Stop talking crazy and listen. No more talk like that, do you hear me?"
He said nothing.

"Listen. I think I know where Maxine is."

That got his attention. "Where? Where is she? Let's go get her, right now."

"I don't know for sure, yet, so I don't want to say. But I'm pretty sure she is fine. Safe and sound. I need to investigate a few other things, but my take is this is all a really bad joke. A few stupid, bored kids pulling a prank."

"Do you know who?" he asked.

"I have some ideas, but I haven't confirmed anything. You need to give me some more time. If it's what I think it is, I need to find those responsible; so, they can be held accountable."

"When you find out, you'll tell me, right?"

"Of course, Luke. Don't be silly. But in the meantime, I need for you to go around and take down all those posters."

Luke squirmed. "But why? I just put them up and I still have more in the truck. I'm not done."

"Luke, you're forgetting one small detail. Most *Wanted Posters* have the picture of the individual that is wanted. Your poster may backfire on you. Not everyone is going to read the fine print. I'm afraid others may only see the big details: *Wanted... Dead or Alive... $100.00... and a picture of Maxine.* Some may go goat hunting."

Luke sat there looking off the porch toward the street. Then he cut a look my way. "You don't actually think that..."

All I did was raise my eyebrows, a gesture that said, *I don't know.*

His eyes cut back to the street, then to his truck. He didn't say another word and darted off the glider, jumped off the porch, right over his overgrown boxwoods, and into the yard. He sprinted toward the truck as his empty glider squealed back and forth. He moves well for an old fart.

I hollered his way, "I'll call you as soon as I know something. And get yourself something to eat, dammit."

My truck had him blocked in, but that didn't stop him. He cut through the yard slinging gravel and grass everywhere fishtailing to the street. Just like that. He was gone.

I remained on the swing to finish my beer, then Luke's. He never took a sip, and if Red ever taught me one thing, it was to never leave a beer to waste away. Afterward, I walked out to my truck and reached behind my seat for my toolbox. As I did, my phone bonged with a text message. It was from Red, four words: *tonight, raw bar, remember.*

I lowered my tailgate and set the toolbox down to open. Under the top tray was exactly what I was looking for. I pulled out a small spray can of white lithium grease and walked back to the porch.

It was 1930 when I arrived at the Forgotten Coast Shrimp and Raw Bar. It was shaping up to be another casual night in a world removed from the stresses that accompany reality. The usual combination of locals and tourists had assembled and gotten a small head start on me. Brian Bowen, our local singer-songwriter and all-around troubadour was getting the crowd on the porch warmed up. He was singing an original cut from his debut CD "There Goes the Neighborhood". I had just been listening to it in the truck, so walking into a live session was a treat.

I mingled outside before going in to look for Red and stake my claim at the bar. At the door I again found myself staring into the eyes of Maxine, another poster. I ripped it down. *Dammit, Luke.*

There were a couple of stools available, but the one right next to the draft beer station caught my eye. It was empty, seventeen written all over it. I sat down, reached to my right and pulled me a Solo cup of Coors Light. I grabbed a big slice of lime and squeezed hard, instant Coorsona.

Bucky Jones was behind the bar. He was shucking oysters like it was nobody's business, earbuds in and iPod blaring. His head was bobbing in time to "Give Me Three Steps," a Lynyrd Skynyrd classic. The whole bar could hear it. He looked at me and offered a wink and a smile. I spoke, but all he saw was my mouth moving. He flipped one bud out of his right ear.

"Huh," he said.

"Buck," I said, "you got to stop listening to your music so damn loud. You're going to screw up your hearing." I scanned the room then asked, "Have you seen, Red? Trixie said he came inside."

Trixie usually does a pretty good job of keeping up with him, but Red can be a slick and greasy one, slipping away unnoticed. He wasn't outside. He wasn't inside. And the guy walking out of the head wasn't a match. *Where in the Hell did he go?*

Rubbing his right thumb and fingers together, eyebrows raised, a sly grin on his face, Bucky asked, "What's it worth to ya?"

"Don't give me any of your crap, Buck. Where's Red?"

"Come on, Mr. Logan. H.B.O., help a brother out."

"What if I buy you a beer?" I said.

"I'm not old enough to drink beer. You know that. You'd be con-tributing to the delinquency of a minor."

"Not really. You're already a delinquent and your age hasn't stopped you from drinking before."

He smiled.

"So, Buck, are you going to tell me where Red is, or am I going to tell Luke McKenzie about what happened to his favorite goat? The real story. The truth. He's pretty upset you know?"

That got Buck's attention. His eyes got wide. He looked from side to side to see if anyone had caught what I said. He leaned forward and tried to whisper but spoke louder than he realized, the music in his earbuds were still way too loud. "What are you talking about?"

I took the picture of Maxine out of my pocket, the one taken by the kidnappers. I unfolded it and showed it to Buck. "Recognize this?"

A nervous twang in his voice he said, "Ah... Sure. That's Maxine. Everybody knows Maxine."

"Not Maxine, Buck. Look again. I'm talking about the class ring."

Buck looked at the picture, then at the ring on his hand, then at the picture again and said, "Oh, shit."

"That's right," I said. "I know everything, Buck. Including everyone involved."

"Who told you? Was it, Sammy?"

I shook my head no.

"Blair?"

"Nope," I said.

I know everything. That wasn't true. I only speculated that Buck and his cronies were involved. I had no proof. It was a hunch until now.

"So, I'm going to ask you one last time. Where is Red?"

"Mr. Logan. You got to understand. We were having a little fun. And now it's gotten all out of hand. The damn goat is crazy."

"Buck. Where's Red?"

"Nigel, please. Have you seen those posters?"

"Buck!"

"He was sitting right there, dammit. The stool you're on now."

"So where did he go?"

"I don't know. Honest. He took a call from his cell phone then got up and left. He said something to me, but I couldn't hear. My music, you know."

"You're no help," I said grabbing my stuff. I recharged my beer and headed to the door.

Bucky's voice followed me. "Mr. Logan. Mr. Logan, listen. We're cool on that other thing, right? Like, no need to worry, huh?"

Without turning around, I said, "That's entirely up to you, Buck. Entirely up to you."

I went out the door.

When I found Red, he was with Trixie out by the smoker; a small fire burned inside. The radiant heat felt good against the warm fall evening, plus it helps keep the no-see-ums away. There were several others too, sampling moonshine from the mountains of North Carolina. As

I walked up, Joe Crow offered me the Ball Mason jar, holding it out in my direction. I declined. *No thanks.*

Trixie had a big smile on her face when she asked, "So Nigel, when is the big date?"

"Huh?" I replied.

"The big date. Your date with Candice, goofball. She says she has finally roped you into a big night out."

"How did you hear about that?"

"Red told me."

Red was chuckling with a less-than-innocent snicker on his face.

"How did you hear about it, Red?"

Before he had a chance to say anything, I held up my hand. "Don't answer that. It doesn't matter. You know everything, but who else knows."

Red said, "Now that Trixie knows, everybody."

Red winced and continued his chuckling as Trixie delivered two quick smacks to his arm. As she reared back and swung for a third shot, he jumped back with a laugh and said, "Come with me, Nigel. Let me give you something before I forget again."

We walked over to his Ford Exploder and he said, "It's not much. A little something for the cottage. A lot of the locals have these. I know Joe does, and I figured you should have one too."

He opened the backseat driver's side door and reached down to the floorboard. He produced a masonry brick and handed it to me. It looked old and had a different look and feel, absent of the traditional three holes. It was solid. I looked at him with a smile and said, "It's a brick, Red. Aww, just what I've always wanted."

"Flip it over and look at the front," he said.

There was the significance. Stamped on the top, were the words *St. Joe.*

"Ah Hell," I said. "That is pretty cool."

Red smiled.

"Did Port St. Joe have a brick company?" I asked.

"No. No. No. These come from Louisiana and are not your typical contractor-grade brick. They're special and made with the traditional wood frame process. Each brick is made that way, no mass production or automated techniques. They're one of the last masonry companies remaining to do so."

"Really?"

"For over 130 years. Look them up. Anyway, here's your St. Joe brick. Display it well."

As I was about to thank Red, we got distracted by the sound of a vehicle sliding sideways to a halt in the middle of the gravel parking lot. It was the truck of Luke McKenzie. We stood there and watched him jump out of the truck and run up and stop at the front door.

Brian Bowen gave him a shout out, cleverly working in a *Hey Luke* in the middle of singing "Troubled Little Souls," another cut from his CD. Given the circumstances, it was a fitting tune for the occasion.

Luke didn't acknowledge Brian. He stood there for a moment looking at the window with his head in his hands, rubbing and pulling his hair. Realizing his poster had already been taken down; he turned tail and ran back to his truck. He had left it running. In one smooth motion he jumped in, slammed the door shut, threw it into drive, and slung gravel as he worked his truck back to the pavement and toward Port St. Joe. He never noticed us as he flew by.

Red said, "That's one disturbed, little old man."

"Yeah. I'd say so. But... he hasn't cut his ear off yet."

We laughed and walked back to the smoker.

The next day I was in my truck sitting at the intersection of Highway 98 and 71. I had my St. Joe brick in the passenger seat, and we were waiting for the light to change. It was the lunchtime rush hour, downtown Port St. Joe. Three cars were in front of me, one behind. A regular traffic jam: it's enough to drive you crazy.

I was headed to the Piggly Wiggly to pick up a few items to provision my cabinets. They had gotten quite sparse over the last week or so and needed restocking.

The light was about to turn green when the honk of a horn got my attention. In the lane next to me I saw Bucky Jones in his old pickup.

His buddy, Sammy Bell, was with him. Bucky motioned for me to roll down my window.

"Mr. Logan," Bucky said. "We need to talk."

"About what?"

"I think you know what," Bucky replied.

The light turned, and I told them to meet me in the parking lot of the Pig.

I parked way out in the back of the lot, got out and leaned up against the driver's side door. Bucky and Sammy pulled in close. I took a hard look at both. Each had their own unique expression of worry. It was time for a little *Come to Jesus*, and they wanted to broker a deal. It was time to pull the plug on their little prank and make everything right with Old Man McKenzie and Maxine.

"Where is Blair?" I asked. "He's a part of this too, is he not?"

Bucky Jones, Sammy Bell, and Blair Stanton were rarely seen apart. They were thick as thieves. When you saw one, you knew the other two were somewhere close. But not today. Bucky and Sammy looked at each other before Sammy said, "We tried to talk to him, but he says he ain't got nothing to talk about."

"Really?" I asked. "That's what he said, huh? How does that make the two of you feel? Letting the both of you take the heat, while he sits back taking no responsibility at all. He's hanging you two out to dry."

"It pisses me off," Bucky said. "The son of a bitch!"

"Well, here's the deal. I'm pretty sure I can make all this go away. Ya hear me?" They both nodded their heads. "But I won't to talk to either of you unless all three of you are here. If you can't get that little dickweed to man up, then I'll have to take everything I know to the authorities and let them sort it all out."

Bucky and Sammy exchanged looks. Then Bucky replied, "We understand. We'll get him. Don't worry."

"I don't have a reason to worry, Buck." I let that sink in as I took a quick look at my watch. It was just before noon. "Get Blair and meet me at Jetty Park in two hours, 1400."

As Bucky rolled up his window, I heard Sammy asked Bucky what fourteen hundred meant. Bucky said, "I don't know, dumbass. We just got to get our asses back here by 2 o'clock." He rolled up the window, and I smiled.

Jetty Park is a neat place. It provides a nice view of the bay and access to the channel leading into the marina. It's a popular spot amongst locals, has a couple of small fishing piers that extend out into the bay, and it's a great place to catch the daily sunset. Several people were fishing the piers and a few more were along the seawall. I watched and determined the catch of the day was Black Drum. Tomorrow it could be something else.

I looked at my watch. It was 1410; they were late. I was sitting on the tailgate. I was patient and figured I'd give them some more time, especially since I would never really turn them over to the authorities, not over something like this. That was a bluff.

I popped a beer, and before I could take a sip, I spotted Bucky's old beach-beater truck coming down the road. The lift kit that jacked up the chassis was worth more than the whole damn truck. It is an old Dodge, red in color, or used to be. Now, it was a pale magenta with plenty of deep, pitted rust, trimming out the wheel wells. It was a thing of beauty to any youngster around these parts.

I counted three heads in the cab. They pulled into the empty spot next to me and parked. They didn't get out. I jumped off the tailgate and walked around to the driver's side window. Bucky rolled down the window and said, "Well, here we are."

Bucky was looking none too happy. He had a puffy lip and his t-shirt was torn at the collar. I looked over at the others. Blair was sitting, sandwiched in the middle. Both he and Sammy were looking straight ahead, neither willing to make eye contact.

I took a hard look at Blair. His lip was fattened up too. Plus, I could tell his nose had been bleeding. When he finally turned his head toward me, I saw his right eye. A big puffy mouse had swollen up underneath, the precursor to one hell of a shiner.

"What happened to you, Blair?"

At first, nobody said anything. Sammy finally turned his head and said, "He fell down."

I smiled. "I see. I see that. We should try to be more careful from now on."

I made a quick assessment and decided further questioning about their current condition wasn't needed. These were three friends; they've known each other probably since they were in diapers. You can't be friends that long and not have been down this road before: A big disagreement, words, an altercation, and a push or two, and finally... fisticuffs.

At that moment, some in the cab hated each other. By this time next week, they'll all be drunk on cheap beer and cast-netting mullet in the surf. It was a classic ritual of rural brotherly love.

I didn't waste any more time. I put on my chief's hat and got right to it.

"Okay, guys," I said. "We are going to put this whole matter to bed today. There will be no discussion. This is a one-way conversation. Are we clear?"

Bucky and Sammy both respectfully replied with a nod of the head and a, "*Yes sir.*" Blair said nothing. That annoyed me.

"Blair?" I asked. "Are we clear on that point? I'm not messing around here."

He slowly turned his head toward me and we locked eyes. What he saw in my eyes, I'm quite sure, was different from what I saw in his. I didn't blink, and he finally turned away nodding his head in agreement.

Luke McKenzie welled up in tears when I told him Maxine had been recovered. She was safe and would soon be returned. He was ecstatic with the news as we sat on the front porch. I was again on the swing, he on the glider that moved with smooth grace, void of squeaks. He didn't notice.

Luke was full of questions. *Where had she been? Had I seen her? How did I know she was safe?* And of course, the biggest question of all. *Who was responsible?*

I told him everything I knew. It was as I suspected; a joke pulled off by local knuckleheads. They never intended for things to get this far out of hand. Once they saw the "Wanted" posters, they froze on what to do next. They got scared and hoped the whole thing would just go away.

"How did you find her?" he asked.

I told him about the picture, the ring, the nests in the trees, and about the drift Red and I took behind Pig Island. "Once all the evidence came together, and I heard her bell clanging from the island, I knew that's where she was."

I left out the part about Red shooting me a big moon, dropping his pants on the boat. It wasn't relevant, and it was an image I was still having a hard time erasing from my memory.

"Where is she now?" asked Luke.

"I'm not exactly sure, but they have her. They sent me a text once they got her off the island."

"Those bastards kept her hostage out on that damn island," he said. Luke was shifting away from the smiles and gleeful excitement and back toward being mad. He considered the conditions on the island to be torturous and miserable for Maxine. "Those sons of bitches!"

Truth is, except for not having access to her room, television, and her nightly beer ritual, she was probably happier than a pig in shit. There is no shortage of food and water on the island. It would have been a big smorgasbord. It's hard to say, though. She really does like her beer.

Luke was turning purple in the face. "Who? Who did it? I want and have a right to know."

I gave him the names. Told him about their original idea. "They wanted to get Maxine and drop her off one night in front of the house. Maybe tie her to a tree, then beat it. I told them that wouldn't be acceptable and that they would need to face you and apologize. And not just an apology, but a public one."

Luke mumbled under his breath, "Little fuckers."

I got off the swing and patted him on the back and said, "Come on. Follow me out to the Raw Bar. That's where they'll be bringing her."

Luke looked up at me. His eyes told me he was ready for this to be over. Then he smiled big and said, "Let me get my coat."

Luke and I got to the Raw Bar first. The kids were nowhere to be found. As we walked to the door, I sent Bucky a text message, no words, only a question mark. I grabbed stool seventeen and Luke took the one to my right. Luke looked around and asked, "Where the hell are they?"

I shrugged my shoulders saying nothing. Then my phone bonged. I looked at the screen. It was a reply from Bucky. I showed the screen to Luke. *Five minutes almost there.* Luke smiled.

"I'm getting a beer, Luke. Want one? My treat."

"No thanks. You've done enough."

I got up and went to the draft station and pulled myself a Coors Light. I took a sip and looked at Luke. He seemed calm, not as nervous or anxious as I would have expected. I watched him as he surveyed the room. I did the same.

It was late afternoon. There were several tourists, but most were locals getting warmed up for a routine night on the porch. I looked toward the front window and saw Sammy heading toward the door; Bucky and Blair brought up the rear.

They came in the door and stopped. I saw Bucky take a deep breath and motioned for the others to follow. Since Bucky works at the Raw Bar, he naturally went behind the counter. Did he do so out of habit or to seek some refuge behind the counter, to put some distance between himself and Luke? My guess would be the latter. Sammy and Blair took up positions by the bar and to the right of Luke.

At first there was silence. It was awkward and Luke allowed it to carry on. Then, Luke said, "Well, where is she?"

The three of them exchanged glances. Bucky spoke first. He was looking at his feet when he said, "She's in the back of the truck, Luke."

I interjected and said, "Look at me Bucky." He did. "You will show Mr. McKenzie some respect, boy."

Bucky said, "Yes, sir. I'm sorry. I mean, she's in the truck, Mr. Luke... Sir."

It got quiet again and finally it was Sammy that grew a set of balls and said, "Mr. McKenzie. I'm sorry about all this. We all are. We never meant to cause any real harm. We just..."

Bucky couldn't stand the idea of Sammy speaking for the group. Buck has always been the front man, and now Sammy was upstaging him. There would be none of that, so Bucky forcefully interrupted. He should have kept his mouth shut because things went downhill from there. Bucky said, "It was a joke, Luke. Sir. That's all it was, just a little joke. No harm, not really."

"A joke, huh?" Luke said with aggravation in his voice. "Really? Like a Ha-Ha kind of joke?"

I could see the worry build in Bucky's eyes. He stumbled with his words, "Well... Umm..."

Luke didn't let up. He raised his voice. "You said it was a joke, you little shit. Tell me, who laughed? Tell me. I want to know."

Bucky said nothing. Luke shared his gaze with all three of them and said, "Come on. I want to know. Funny jokes are meant to be shared. Who heard about this one?"

Again, it was Sammy stepping up to the plate. He said, "We didn't tell anyone, sir. It was only us three that knew."

Luke asked Sammy, "What about you? Did you laugh? Did you find it funny?"

Sammy dropped his head and stared at his feet. Blair said nothing. He never offered an apology or anything. He remained stoic and silent like he wasn't involved. Luke gave him a hard look in the eye. Nothing was there but icy indifference.

Luke had worked himself into a controlled frenzy. I'd seen it a hundred times. He had returned to his old Navy roots. A brother chief was putting his hat on and preparing to deliver one hell of an ass chewing. Luke turned back to Bucky and said, "Maybe I was supposed to find it all funny. Is that it, you little prick?" Luke looked up at the ceiling tiles in thought and said, "I can hear it now, 'That Old Man McKenzie, he'll think this is funny as shit.' Is that how it went?"

Bucky said, "Please Luke, calm down."

That was the wrong thing to say because that's when Luke produced a Colt, nickel-plated 38 Special from his right coat pocket and pointed it at Bucky. *Oh Shit!*

The commotion had already drawn the attention of everybody in the place, but when the gun came out, it was a game-changer. All the tourists took to the door and exited in a hurry. The locals backed off a bit and gave the situation a wide berth, but they didn't leave.

Bucky's hands went up with a gasp, as did the other two. Even Blair joined in with a girlish squeal. If he wasn't taking the situation seriously before, he was now.

Fear can have a strange effect on people. It also can bring out a person's true character. While Bucky and Blair whimpered and pleaded, it was Sammy that again collected enough courage to speak.

Sammy said, "Mr. McKenzie. Please. Please put the gun away. I beg of you. We did a very stupid thing, and we are sorry. We'll do whatever it takes to make this up to you. Maxine is safe and in the truck. We've learned our lesson. Please."

I was standing right there. I could see the back of the cylinder; there were bullets in the chambers. I was getting nervous. I got close and spoke to Luke in a calm and quiet voice. "What are you doing, Luke? This is no way of handling this. You've put plenty of scare in them. Now do me a favor and put the gun away. Let's get Maxine and go home."

"He told me to calm down," Luke said. "Like he has the right to tell me to do anything. I've been a wreck since this whole thing started, and he's going to tell me to calm down. Screw him."

Then everybody's sphincter puckered up a little tighter when Luke pulled back and locked the hammer.

"Chief." I said raising my voice, one retired CPO to another. "Come on now. Knock this shit off. You don't want to do this. Trust me, I know."

Luke cut his eyes toward me. He heard what I said and was now giving me a surprised and confused look. I could be wrong, but I swear I noticed a slight relaxation and lowering of the gun. But what I heard next had to be the dumbest thing to ever come out of anyone's mouth.

I don't know what it is about being young and dumb. I guess we all were, but some folks never fail to amaze me. He hadn't said a thing the entire afternoon. He just stood there looking inconvenienced until compelled to lift his hands high at the sight of the gun, a mere spectator until now. In his infamous wisdom and overwhelming stupidity, Blair Stanton spoke.

My eyes grew wide when Blair said, "Mr. McKenzie! Really? All this over a fucking goat!"

Any relief Bucky felt when Luke swung the pistol away from him and toward Blair immediately turned into a nightmare. Everything that happened next came and went in a flash. I wasn't fast enough to stop it.

When close to gunfire, you don't hear it; you feel it. It has a paralyzing effect. You freeze, especially when the circumstances are so dramatic and violent. I felt helpless.

The first rounds were unloaded into Blair's chest. Three shots, center mass. Blair screamed and clutched at his chest as he fell backward bouncing off a table and onto the floor.

Luke turned to Bucky. I heard Bucky plead for his life and call out for his Momma, but Luke popped two quick rounds. Bucky gasped and hollered as he spun around, thrown back against the sink.

By the time Luke turned the gun on Sammy, the boy was already down on his knees, in shock, looking at the floor and waiting his turn. It never came. Expecting at any moment to feel his life slip away, all he heard was *click, click, click*. Luke spent his rounds on Blair and Bucky, but that didn't stop Luke from searching for one more round. *Click! Click! Click!* He kept pulling the trigger.

The chaos was highlighted by the continued screams for help and the hollering of Bucky and Blair. Everyone was in disbelief of what they had just witnessed. Once I finally came out of my state of paralysis, I walked up to Luke and reached out and carefully took the gun from his hand asking, "Oh my God, Luke. What have you done?"

"Nothing," he said with a stone-cold grin. "Ain't no big deal."

Luke started yelling at the kids. "Get up, you bunch of pussies. Stop your bellyaching. You ain't shot." Luke looked back at me with a big smile and said, "Blanks."

Luke walked over to Blair and gave him a swift kick. "Get up jackass. Your dumbass days ain't over yet."

He walked over toward Bucky, "Same for you, dipshit. All three of you, get up and come here."

In a confused panic, riddled with relief and astonishment, they stood shaking from the excitement. You could tell they wanted out of there. They didn't want to spend one more minute in Luke's presence. Blair was still feeling his chest to make sure he hadn't really been shot. Sammy stood there, turned to the side, looking at the floor. He had pissed his pants and was doing his best to hide.

Bucky yelled, his voice shaking, "That was crazy. No. No. You, you're crazy. You're a crazy old coot."

"Shut your hole, boy."

Luke stood there looking at all three of them. They were shaking like leaves trying to free themselves from a branch on a cold, windy day. Then Luke spoke, "What's the matter? Didn't you find that funny? It was a little joke. I thought you boys liked a good joke."

At that moment, all the built-up tension in the folks that had witnessed the events turned to belly-busting laughter. I had never seen such a shift in emotions. Everyone went from incredible tragedy to joyous cacophony. I guess you could add extreme embarrassment if you add in how the boys were feeling.

Addressing the boys over the laughter, Luke said, "So, I'm guessing we won't have any more trouble out of you three for a while. I think we can consider this matter closed. What do you think?"

All three nodded in agreement.

"Very good then! We have an accord."

Luke shook each of their hands to seal the deal. When he got to Sammy, he held his hand a bit longer. He maintained his grip until their eyes met. Luke told him, "You did fine today, son." Sammy nodded back. Then Luke concluded, noticing Sammy had wet his pants, "But you'll want to do something with those britches. You don't want to get caught with a rusty zipper."

He released Sammy's hand and said, "Now y'all get!"

They didn't waste a second. They scattered like spooked quail. As we watched them hightail it to the door, our attention got diverted. Standing inside the door was Red, smiling big. He had Maxine on a leash. In grand celebration, Red said, "Look what I found!"

Luke took off toward the door and Red turned Maxine loose. They met each other in the middle of the room. It was peculiar to see how excited they were to see each other, especially Maxine. She was like a faithful, loving dog meeting its master after an extended period of separation.

Red walked over to me. We watched their little reunion until it got a little uncomfortable. Still watching, Red leaned his head toward me and with a slight grimace said, "Kind of strange, huh?"

"Yeah, a little weird, borderline perverted. Maybe they need to get a room."

Red chuckled. Then, loud enough for the room to hear, said, "Hey! Somebody buy that old girl a beer, she has to be one thirsty goat."

BROWN

If you hang around on the Forgotten Coast long enough, there is no telling what will cross your path, even a memory, one long since dismissed as unimportant. All it takes is the proper stimuli to pull those lost experiences to the forefront of your mind, as if it all happened yesterday. Recently, it happened to me. Someone from my past walked through the front door of the Forgotten Coast Shrimp and Raw Bar and back into my brain.

"Well, I'll be damned," I said, after washing a salty Apalachicola oyster down with my cold beer.

"What?" Red asked.

My buddy Red and I were sitting at the bar. Bucky, our favorite shucker, was bobbing his head to the music in his earbuds and cracking shells to keep our tray full. Locals don't order by the dozen. We sit down and start eating. When you finish, you get a shell count and pay the resident price at the register. It doesn't get much easier than that.

I looked at Red and thumbed toward a guy at the door and said, "That poor bastard. His name is Melvin."

Red gave him a full inspection. Melvin came in with a woman, presumably his wife, and two kids. They looked quite touristy. It was obvious they hadn't been in town long. If I had to guess, they were coming off their first beach day. Small portions of their skin were still pasty white, while others were burnt to a blood-red hue. All of them, kids included, moved with great, deliberate care.

Red looked back my way and said, "Okay... I'll bite. What's the story? How do you know him?"

"Navy boot camp," I said. "I wonder if he'll recognize me. Damn, that was what, over twenty-five years ago?"

"And if he recognized you?" Red asked.

"It's hard to say," I replied.

Like most, I started my naval service in Great Lakes, Illinois. Unlike most others, I entered service a little older. I was well into my twentieth year when I raised my hand to swear in. On my twenty-first birthday, I stood the mid-watch in the barracks, midnight to four hundred hours. I relieved the watch fifteen minutes early, a traditional courtesy for all watchstanders. And, as the clock struck twelve, I entered the occasion of my birthday in the logbook in huge, block lettering known as *Ricky Writing*.

It was a huge *no-no* to include non-significant details in a Navy logbook. I knew I would suffer some consequences, but I didn't care. What would a few extra push-ups mean to me? I stood at six foot three inches and carried a solid 200 lb frame, a body prepared for punishment. It didn't intimidate me. I knew boot camp was mostly a mind game, anyway. Designed as an emotional roller coaster with valuable lessons inserted along the way. A truly masterful program honed to perfection over years of experience.

The next morning the entire company was standing at attention, waiting for the morning inspection. We were crisp and clean, the tips of our polished boondockers shined behind a straight seam of blue tiling. Our Company Commander, a Chief, exited his office and slammed his door. From the corner of my eye, I could see the logbook in his hand. *Here we go.*

The Chief went into a rant as he marched up and down the aisle. He was furious, telling us about the seriousness of keeping appropriate and accurate logs, that it was a historical document often used in courts to recollect specific details about a ship's activities. All true. Then he stopped in front of me and placed his nose two inches away from mine and yelled, "Not to record your cheery, fucking birthday wishes, Logan!" He was loud, very loud. His spit hit me in the face. I stood and took it. It was punishment time.

No big deal. A few extra push-ups meant nothing. They would be worth it. When he said, "Hit the deck!" I was down in the position with one sweeping motion: head looking forward, hands shoulder-width apart, feet together, back straight. Then Chief got on his hands and knees to look me square in the eye and said, "Not you, Logan."

Pointing and waving his index finger up and down the barracks aisle, he said, "Them."

I turned my head and looked down the line at my shipmates, their faces full of sudden worry and anxiety. It was brilliant. He wasn't interested in hurting me physically; the chief wanted to hit me mentally, make me watch my shipmates endure an unwarranted punishment and instill an overwhelming guilt in my mind. *You asshole.*

I stayed in the push-up position and protested. "Sir! No, sir! This has nothing to do with them, sir! It wouldn't be right, sir!"

Chief said, "It wasn't right for you to molest and diminish the integrity of the logbook, Logan. And you're all a team, right? What's good for one is good for..." He let the rest fade away.

"Sir. Permission to speak freely, sir," I said.

"On your feet, Logan."

In almost the same smooth motion, in reverse, I was back at attention. Chief got back in my face and glared at me with his usual snarl. Bottom lip poked out for effect. I spoke. "Chief, sir. I take full responsibility for my actions, sir. Isn't that what we're supposed to do? My shipmates played no part in my logbook entry. I acted by myself. What do they call it... unilaterally? They are all innocent, sir."

I saw the Chief's mood swing a bit. His bottom lip pulled back into place. "They're all innocent?" he asked. "Every single one of them? Is that what you're telling me?"

"Well... yes, sir. I acted alone."

The Chief shook his head from side to side. "Aside from all that," he said. "Forget the logbook. Are they all innocent?"

I couldn't understand the context of his question. There had to be one, so I answered best I could. "Well, sir. I guess not. We are all guilty of something, of one thing or another. My father always said we're an imperfect species, sir."

The Chief thought that over as he walked up and down the line looking at my shipmates. He stepped back in front of me and asked, "So, you would feel bad if I made everybody do push-ups?"

"Yes, sir. It wouldn't be right."

"Well, somebody's got to do some push-ups, dammit."

"They're my push-ups, sir. I'm ready."

"No." The Company Commander said, "I like the idea of making you watch."

Crap.

"Pick one. Pick one of your shipmates, Logan. You get to decide who does your push-ups. That's the way this is going to go down."

Son of a bitch. He wanted me to turn on one of my shipmates, another clever tactic. He turned away and got in the face of Jerry Wilson. We call him Hulaco, after the small community he's from in north Alabama. "What about Wilson, here?" Then he spoke to Wilson, saying, "You wouldn't mind doing a few push-ups for Logan, would you?"

I turned and looked at a very nervous Hulaco. His face twitched with anxiety, not knowing if he should speak. I spoke and got him off the hook.

"No, sir," I said. "Wilson is a good shipmate, sir. He helps Taylor with his studies. Not that Taylor is dumb or anything. It's just that..."

The chief cut me off, and said, "Well, if not Wilson..." He stepped away and turned and crossed the aisle. "What about Michaels here? He's nothing but a SLUFF."

SLUFF, an acronym for *Short Little Ugly Fat Fucker*. I smiled and, with a slight chuckle, said, "No, sir. He's working hard to lose that extra fat. He still has a few pounds to go, but he's going to make weight by graduation. Just you wait and see, sir."

Then the chief stepped away and came back to me. We were face to face. He said nothing, looked into my eyes, and conveyed a silent message with a small smile. *Pick one.*

Then I realized. He was allowing me to isolate someone. He wanted me to pick a bug, a dysfunctional member of the unit, someone we all would take pleasure in seeing do push-ups. They would be undeserving push-ups, but not totally. The chief's words came back to me. *They're all innocent? Every single one of them?*

I didn't have to think long before a name popped into my head, Melvin Brown. Brown was from Detroit and a piece of work. I didn't like him or his attitude. He always did the very minimum and flew just under the radar of trouble. If there was some problem within the company, he was somewhere close to the fire. If there was a shortcut, he took it. He wasn't a team player and thought only of himself. He never helped his other shipmates in need. And he always looked like shit in his uniform. While the rest of us ironed and creased our dungaree shirts, his minimum but passing standard of uniform preparation looked like ass in comparison.

As I stood at attention thinking of all the perfect reasons to mention Melvin's name, the bottom lip of the chief swelled again. Then, he yelled, "Goddammit! Pick somebody, Logan. We're all getting hungry. You're going to make us miss chow. Now quit screwing around and pick one."

I stood at attention, eyes straight, with a hard, focused look. I asked, "What color is shit, sir?"

The chief shook his head in anger. "What did you say? What the hell is that supposed to mean, Logan?"

He got in my face again, closer than before. His breath smelled of cigarettes and coffee. Before he was about to let me have it, I spoke again. "Shit, sir. What color is it?"

At that moment, the light came on. He backed off with a smile, a smile only I could see. It was another silent message. Maybe it was, *I like you, kid,* or... *you're going to be just fine in this man's Navy.* But I think it was more like *that would have been my choice too.*

I asked one more time, and the chief backed off a few steps and jumped all over me, "What do you think I am, Logan, stupid? Is that what you are saying? Everybody knows the color of shit. It's Brown!"

They were the easiest 75 push-ups I've ever had to watch another person do. Poor bastard.

No Cream ... No Sugar

I looked at my hand, then at the pot of money. It was fat with cash. I looked at my hand and liked my chances but didn't want to look too eager. I wanted to frustrate everyone with my indecisiveness, play it dumb, which is the way most of my poker playing is done, anyway. I wanted to appear confused, to expose my inexperience. *Stay in or fold?* There was no confusion; I was all in, regardless.

"It's to you, Nigel," said Joe Crow.

I looked up and around the room at the other players around the table. They were all looking at me, growing more impatient. "I know. I know. Give me a minute," I said.

Red said, "Giving you a minute to look at your cards is like spending the night in jail. Morning never seems to come."

From straight across the table, Michael Bobo said, "Come on, Nigel. Are you in or out? My hand is getting cold."

"Come on, Mike," I said. "Quit busting my chops, dammit."

Mike Bobo owns the Gulf Shrimp Company and has a fleet of boats. Although he is the CEO, it's in name only. He turned the everyday operation of the company over to his daughter. Mike isn't a salesman, nor is he the desk jockey office type. His heart is in the boats. And if he's going to be in the shrimping business, he's going to do it from the wheelhouse, not a telephone. He skippers the *Miss Cecilia*, named for his little girl that now runs the company.

I slid my cards to the edge of the table and bent the ends up taking another look. Red was humming the theme song to Jeopardy. I cut him an *eat shit* look.

I took another look at the cards, put them down, and threw my chips in the middle. "Okay. Crap, I guess I'm in!"

The sigh that was heard around the table said, *it's about time.*

The bets went around the table one last time. Then it came time to air out the laundry, hang it out there, and show everybody their goods. I had a queen-high straight, my best hand ever. I had bested everyone at the table, but Red hadn't shown his cards yet.

"Well," Mike said. "Cough 'em up, Red. It's show time."

"Hold on a second," Red said. "I'm not feeling so good."

I looked over at Red. His head was drooped over the table. He didn't look well at all, terrible. He looked dizzy and out of sorts, even unstable as he wobbled around in his chair.

I said, "Red. Brother. You, Okay?"

"Yeah. I think so," he said. "I'm feeling a little..." Then he picked up his cards and threw them on the table and yelled with great laughter, "Flushed!"

Sure enough, he had five hearts of varying varieties.

"Son... of... a... bitch!" I said.

Joe said, "I saw that coming."

The table busted out in laughter. Mike slapped his hand on the table and yelled, "Sucker!"

"Ya'll knew? Ya'll knew he was going to do that?" I asked.

Laughing, Joe said, "It was only a matter of time. It happens, eventually, to every new guy at the table."

As Red smiled and pulled his chips over to his side of the table, I said, "Ya'll are a bunch of assholes, but I wouldn't trade you for the world."

We all laughed as I gathered the cards. It was my turn to deal. We were taking verbal jabs and stabs at one another. As I shuffled, a phone rang. It was Mike's. He looked at the screen and stood saying, "It's Cecilia. I need to take this."

I took extra care to shuffle the deck as we waited on Mike. Red got up to get everybody a fresh beer, and Joe counted his chips. He had done well and got that *stop while I'm ahead* look in his eye.

Mike came back to the table and said, "I got to leave. Trouble on the boat that I need to handle before the morning."

"Sinking?" Red chuckled.

"No, personnel problem. I'm short-handed for tomorrow."

"Short-handed," I said. "That can't be good."

"I'm going to be down a guy. He's had a death in the family. With as healthy as the drags have been, it's going to put one hell of a strain on the rest of the guys."

"Hell, Mike," I said, "I'll come along and give you a hand. I've never been shrimping, but I'm no stranger to boats. Surely there is something I can do to lend a hand."

"I appreciate that Nigel, but shrimp'n is tough and messy. I'm not sure it's for you."

"Damn, Mike, I'm not asking for a job. I'm willing to give you a hand, step in and help take the load off the other guys. Hell, I think it would be kind of fun."

Mike laughed at that.

"What's so funny?" I asked.

"Nothing really," Mike said snickering. "It's just that nobody has ever left the boat after their first day and proclaimed it *a bunch of fun*. It's tough and physical. By the time you're done with the day, you're pretty well exhausted."

"I can appreciate that, but I'm not afraid of a little hard work. Kind of used to it, actually."

"Plus, the crew can be a little rough on a new guy. They don't extend a lot of mercy because it's your first day. It would be initiation by fire. I always tell the new guys to expect it and that I simply have too much going on in the wheelhouse to police the antics of the crew."

"Mike... listen... I'm willing to help. I'm a retired Navy Chief: tested, selected, and initiated. I think I can take care of myself. The offer remains open. It's on the table. Just let me know."

Mike thanked me, cashed in his chips, said good night, and hit the door. The rest of the guys called it a night as well. That was fine with me since my pile of chips had well been exhausted. Without a good streak of luck, I only had enough for a couple of more hands.

When I got back to my house, a strange cat, a dark gray tabby, was at the back door. It was sitting on the top step as if it belonged there. It didn't. I knew most of the cats on my street, but I didn't recognize this one.

"Now, where in the world did you come from?" I asked. It replied with a short meow.

I approached the stoop. The cat didn't have a collar on, but few of the local cats do. I chased it off with a gentle shoo and watched it as it ran around the side of the house.

I was emptying my pockets on the kitchen counter when my phone rang. The Caller ID read, *Mike Bobo*.

"Hello, Mike. What's up?"

"Were you serious about getting underway and helping on the boat?"

"Hell Mike. I wouldn't have offered if I wasn't serious."

"Well, it turns out I may need to impose on you after all, if you don't mind. I'm still short and most of the other guys I've called are too drunk to make boat time or not answering their phones. I'll pay you. Wouldn't ask you to do it for free."

I laughed and said, "You're damn right you're going to pay me. You bastards clean me out at the poker table every night. I need to get my money back somehow. What is boat time?"

"We shove off at 5 am, so if you can be at the boat an hour early, that would be great. I'll pour us a hot cup of coffee and show you around the boat."

I got up at 0330, put on some coffee and took a quick shower. I poured a huge cup to go and left. The early morning air was clean and clear. It was pitch dark. I was half startled when I felt something nudge my ankle. I jumped back a step and opened the door of my truck. The interior light revealed the cat from the night before. It was rubbing up against my shoes and legs. I reached down and picked it up.

Rubbing its head, I asked the cat again. "Now, where in the hell did you come from?"

The cat said nothing. It tilted its head and pressed hard against my hand. I put the cat down and shooed it away. "Go on now. Go back to where you belong. I have work to do."

I showed up wearing an old Navy t-shirt, a pair of bibs from an old set of foul weather gear, and Topsiders. The boat shoes were an old favorite but not long for this world. They were incredibly comfortable and showed years of faithful service by their weathered leather tops. The bibs were still serviceable but heavily worn in areas, the memory in the elastic suspenders all but gone. The t-shirt had seen better days, and I had kept it around for such an occasion, one last hurrah.

Prepared to get nasty, I brought a change of clothes. Nothing I wore on the boat was expected to get past the garbage can as I left, except for maybe the shoes. It's difficult to part with an old pair of Sperry's. No matter how worn they are, throwing them away is like saying goodbye to an old friend.

Mike met me at the dock with a hot cup of coffee, as promised. He took a couple of steps back and looked me over. He gazed at my shoes and said, "I didn't figure you'd have any Reeboks. What size you wear?"

"Reeboks?"

"Yeah. What size?"

"A thirteen, but Reeboks?"

Mike waved for me to follow. We went through the office and into a storage room. He rifled through several boxes before declaring, "Ah ha! Here we go."

He pulled out an old pair of rubber boots. I could see they'd once been snow white but had long since taken on the tones of a lifetime of shrimp'n and fish'n.

Mike said, "St. Joe Reeboks. They were my dad's. Don't muck them up."

"They look like they've been through hell."

"Well, that's the point. You don't want to show up at the boat with a brand-new shiny pair. That would make you stand out too much, make you look like a greenhorn rookie."

"But I am a greenhorn rookie. And I'm comfortable with that."

"Trust me. It is best this way."

I put the stained and weathered boots on and placed my worn-out Topsiders in my dry bag. *There you go, my old friend. You live to walk another day.*

We walked down toward the boat. I saw two deckhands working and making final preparations to get underway. Mike first introduced me to Phil Stewart. Phil is Mike's lead deckhand.

"Phil, come here a minute."

Phil dropped the line he was flaking on deck and walked over.

"I guess you know by now we're short-handed. Ken can't make it. An emergency. He said a death in the family."

Phil looked at me hard with an unwelcoming expression. I continued to smile. *Damn, is that genuine anger in his eyes, or is he just screwing with my head?* He said nothing for a beat or two, then turned to Mike and said, "Family emergency, my ass. Ken got drunk last night. Besides, both his parents are already taking a dirt nap, so I can't imagine who else could have croaked to give him enough reason to miss work."

I looked over at Mike and asked with a grin, "He's a real charmer, isn't he?"

Phil said with a gruff, "I'm none of your goddamn business. That's who I am." He looked at Mike and asked, "What the hell is he doing here?"

Mike looked at me confused and asked, "Ya'll know each other?"

I shook my head no.

Mike interjected, "Phil, meet Nigel Logan. He's going to lend a hand today. He knows his way around a boat but nothing 'bout shrimp'n, so give him the quick tour and use him where you see fit."

"Whatever, Skip." Phil shrugged his shoulders and went back to his duties.

Mike pointed to the other guy, a tall, lanky kid. He looked to be in his early twenties, sported a bad haircut and a severe case of acne. He was standing at the edge of the boat, leaning up against a swab when Mike pointed and said, "And that one there is K.C."

K.C. waved back with a big grin. Happy enough.

I waved back with a smile.

"He's from Mississippi. Was in the Navy for a short while, stationed in Panama City, but they processed him out on a drug charge."

"What drug? Ya know?"

"Pot," Mike said. "I told him I'd have none of that around here and he told me not to worry. Said he was innocent and has never touched the stuff."

"K.C., huh? What's that stand for?"

Mike looked at me with a blank stare, and I saw the corners of his mouth droop. His body language said, *Really? Do you have to ask? Isn't K.C. enough?*

I raised my eyebrows. *Well?*

With an exaggerated look of seriousness, Mike said, "Karl."

"Okay," I said, "how about the last name?"

Mike got quiet and looked around, ignoring me. He didn't want to establish direct eye contact. Mike repeated his first name.

"I get that," I said. "Karl. Karl is the first name. What's his last name?"

With a big grin, Mike again repeated his first name.

"Mike, you're not making a lick of sense. What is this, a bad rendition of Abbott and Costello's, *Who's on first?*"

With a slight laugh, Mike said, "His first and last name are the same. First name with a K, last name with a C."

"You have got to be kidding me?" I asked.

"Nope. That's why we call him K.C."

"Karl Carl? You're serious?"

Mike nodded his head yes, holding back the laughter.

I looked over at K.C. He had returned to his swabbing duties. Skinny and absent of coordination, it was hard to tell if he was controlling the swab or if the swab was controlling him.

I turned back to Mike, lowered my voice, and said, "This kid is screwed."

Mike nodded his head and replied, "From the get-go. Good worker, though."

I found Phil in the galley, pouring a cup of coffee. I asked if he would top me off, but he looked at me with contempt and put the pot back on the burner. *Okay*, I thought, *if that's the way you want to play it*. I poured my own.

I tried to keep the conversation light, so I asked, "How long have you been working with Mike?" It was clear, for whatever reason, my presence wasn't appreciated, so I thought it best to be careful with my words. Working *with* is a lot less insulting than working *for*.

Phil said nothing at first. There was only an awkward silence, but I remained patient. Then he said, "Ten years."

"Wow. That's a long time."

"You two seem mighty chummy. You and Skip, that is."

"We play poker occasionally," I said, smiling. "I show up, and he and the others take my money."

"Skip's never asked me to play poker."

That created another awkward moment. I wasn't sure how to reply, so I ignored it and changed the subject. "What about that quick tour?" I asked.

"Skip says you know your way around a boat. What kinds?"

"All kinds," I said. "Retired Navy."

"Navy, huh? Well, this ain't no battleship, Bucko."

Still trying to keep things friendly, I said, "That's a good thing. I've never been stationed on a battleship, so little good it would have done me anyway, huh? And the name is Nigel. Let's keep things informal, first names."

Phil gave me the Reader's Digest version of a shrimp boat. He showed me around but provided little explanation. What he showed me I could have figured out on my own by looking around.

He showed me the primary winch in the middle of the deck, the outriggers, the large rectangle panels called doors, and the nets that were draped high in the rigging. He showed me the ice machine and said I would become quite familiar with it. For the most part, the tour was worthless.

As we pulled out into the channel, the sea conditions were calm, but the boat rocked more than I would have expected. Once we cleared the Highway 98 bridge and steamed toward the gulf, K.C. lowered the outriggers so they reached horizontally port and starboard over the water. With the rig stretched out, they worked like the long pole of a tightrope walker, making the ride much more stable.

I was leaning up against the stern railing. The fantail. K.C. joined me and we talked over the rumble of the powerful diesels and stern wash that churned behind the boat. I asked, "So what's your story? Skip tells me you were in the Navy. Me too. A chief, retired. How long were you in?"

I didn't let on that Mike had told me about his troubles. I figured if he wanted to volunteer those details, he could on his terms. And if he did, I could better determine if he was lying about it or not. The truth is easier to detect during a casual conversation as opposed to a direct question.

K.C. said, "I was only in for about two and a half years. They gave me a general discharge a few months back on a drug charge. Pot."

"Ouch," I said. "I've seen pot ruin many good Navy careers. There's no room in the fleet for that stuff."

"Oh, I agree."

"Well, if you agree, why were you getting high?"

"I wasn't. That's the thing. I never have. I think they set me up, intentionally fed brownies laced with something. Pot, I guess, since that's what they say was in my system."

He told me about how he didn't get along with the others in his shop, how they constantly picked on and took advantage of him. All he wanted was to fit in, so when they asked him to a party off base, he immediately accepted. He said, "I should have known something was up. They were acting so friendly the entire week."

"So, you think it was the guys in your shop?"

"That's all I can figure. The party was at somebody's house I didn't know. I had a few beers, but that's about it. Then the brownies came out of the oven. They smelled too good to resist."

"Did the guys from your shop eat the brownies too?"

"I can't remember." K.C. thought it over for a few moments and finally said, "You know... I don't think so. I don't even remember seeing them around at that point. The only thing I remember is sitting in a big chair, afraid to get up. Everybody was looking and talking about me. Or at least, it seemed that way."

"How did you get back to the base?"

"A cab. Somebody called it for me, I guess. I don't remember much after that. The next morning, I was called to the Master at Arms shack and given a cup to piss in. The rest is history."

I believed him, every word. I've seen the Navy environment he described, but not to that extreme. It is common for the new guy to take some lumps on their way to fitting in, just like on a shrimp boat. It isn't hazing, more of a trial by fire indoctrination into the Navy. It can be unforgiving and tough. To make it, you must learn how to take it. In learning to take it, you learn how to give it back, too. Unfortunately, K.C. never picked up on the last lesson.

I didn't want to dwell on the subject, so I ended the conversation by asking, "K.C., your chief, the one from your old shop. What's his name?"

He told me.

Phil stepped out of the cabin door and hollered, "You girls want to get off your ass and do some work? K.C., get the doors ready, dammit. We'll be making our first run soon."

K.C. explained that the doors, which... well... look like two big wooden front doors, are hoisted out to the end of the outriggers. There are two of them per side.

K.C. said, "Once the doors are in place, we hoist the nets out to them. The nets are sort of rectangular at the mouth and funnel back to a round catch tube. Skip calls that the money catcher. The doors work like weighted fins. They sink and fan the net's mouth wide open across the bottom."

I was enjoying this. I got the impression that, for once, K.C. enjoyed having a greenhorn shrimper aboard and was getting to play the role of mentor, showing off his knowledge and understanding of the boat. This kid was alright.

I looked over at the cabin and saw Phil leaning up against the doorway. He was being worthless and doing an excellent job. I called out, "Hey Phil, come over here. This kid is great. You might learn something."

Phil grunted and rolled his eyes as he disappeared into the cabin. I looked at K.C. He was grinning and said, "You ought not talk to Phil that way. He'll get mad."

"He can get mad all he wants," I replied. "I don't give a shit."

K.C. said nothing.

"Listen... life at sea isn't easy. It doesn't matter if you are in the Navy, the merchant marines, or working a commercial fishing vessel like the *Miss Cecelia* here, if you are going to make it, grow some thicker skin."

K.C. said nothing.

"Sure, the new guy always has to take their lumps in the beginning. It's the way it is. But if you work hard, prove your salt, and establish yourself as reliable, you won't have to take a bunch of crap from anyone. You better learn to dish it back out as much as the next guy."

He smiled at the thought of that.

"For right now, to hell with Phil. He isn't interested in showing me how this operation rolls or helping, so it's up to you. What do we do next?"

We went over to the nets, two huge jokers, port and starboard. The ends of the catch tubes were open. "This is where the money dumps out," he said with a smile as he closed the first one using a multiple series of looping half hitches.

"Is that secure enough?" I asked. "It doesn't seem very strong."

"Oh, it's strong enough. But the cool thing is, once we get the catch on board and hoisted over the deck, we yank on this bitter end of line and it comes untied, easy like. Shrimp and everything else spilling out on the deck. You'll see."

K.C. inspected my work as I tied up the other net. As we turned around, Phil was standing there. He looked over my handiwork and then at me. "That trip line better be secure."

I didn't reply.

"K.C., get me another cup of coffee."

K.C. didn't hesitate. He grabbed Phil's empty cup and headed toward the galley. I watched him leave and duck through the cabin door. As soon as he was gone, I turned to Phil and asked, "I'm curious. Is there a particular reason you are being such a dick? Or am I lucky and caught you on a good day? I would have thought you'd appreciate having another willing hand on board."

"Screw you. I don't like you."

"You turd. You don't even know me. I'm a guy here to help."

"I'll say it again. Screw you! And yeah, I know who you are, and if you weren't friends with Skip, I'd..." He let his words fall off, realizing he had probably already said too much.

"Really? You'd do what?" With my arms spread out and my palms up, I said, "Don't let Skip stop you."

He glared at me, turned away, and left. *What is this guy's deal?* I stood my ground, letting him brush by as he said, "Just stay out of my way."

I turned to watch him leave and said, "Don't worry. I will. As soon as I see you do something."

K.C. came out on deck, oblivious to the exchange Phil and I just had, but could tell something wasn't right by the awkward look on Phil's face. Phil grabbed his coffee and walked away without even a word of thanks. K.C. walked up.

"Is he always a jerk like this?" I asked.

"Pretty much. Some of the older guys that have been here for a long time say he's been this way since his wife left him. Today seems to be worse than others, though."

"It's me," I said. "For some reason, he's got a stiff one for me."

"Why?"

"I do not know and really don't care."

We were interrupted by the boat's horn, two long blasts. I looked at K.C. and he smiled. "That's our signal," he said. "Skip wants the nets out. Time for our first run."

With the doors and the mouth of the net hoisted out to the outriggers, we fed the net overboard, port and starboard. With everything in place, K.C. lowered the doors into the water. As the doors fought against water and the trolling speed of the boat, they spread the net wide open and sank, maximizing them to their fullest catch potential.

The mouth of the net is rectangular and outfitted with floats along the top edge to provide buoyancy while the bottom edge is weighted. The doors and the bottom of the net work together to keep the net open wide and the bottom edge of the net against the bottom where the money swims. Just forward of the net is a trip chain that runs the entire length of the net's mouth. It skims the sea floor, making the shrimp jump up off the bottom and right into the oncoming net and the catch tube.

We finished our first drag and hauled in the nets. The doors were winched back up to the outriggers and the nets lifted high over the deck of the boat. It was in incredible sight. The first net was packed, but it wasn't until K.C. jerked on the bag line, spilling the contents on the deck that I could appreciate the load.

Everything caught in the net scattered about on deck. There were blue crabs, catfish, a variety of small fish, a few flounder, stingrays, and, of course, shrimp, lots and lots of shrimp. K.C. looked over at me and hollered, "cha-ching," as he pantomimed pulling a lever on an old cash register. At his young age, I wondered if he had ever seen one, an old cash register. Did he really understand what that arm motion meant, or was it something he picked over the years, mimicking the acts of others? I was willing to bet the latter.

It was time to cull through the catch, sort through what needed to be kept and what needed to be returned to the sea. I looked at K.C. and said, "Where do we start?"

He said, "You worry about the bycatch, the trash fish. And I'll start by gathering the shrimp. Keep the big crabs. Put them in a basket. At least five inches wide, tip to tip. We'll collect and take 'em to market too."

It was slow going at first. I've never had to catch a stingray off the deck of a boat before and I've never had the pleasure of being tagged by one. I wanted to keep it that way.

I must have thrown back every type of fish and creature that swims the Gulf of Mexico. With both catch bags emptied on deck and the bigger fish back in the water, I helped K.C. pick the shrimp from the smaller trash fish on deck. I grabbed an empty basket and got after it. As we were clearing the catch, the doors and nets were lowered again to start another run.

I looked up. Phil was leaning against the big winch, arms crossed, watching. The catch was huge. There was still plenty of shrimp on deck and Phil didn't raise a finger except to bark, "Logan. Get those baskets in the hold and ice down that shrimp."

I did as I was told. I didn't mind. That's what I was there for, but to see us do all the work while he stood there was more than a little annoying. I hurried back to help K.C., and asked, "Does he ever help cull through the catch?"

"Only when it's just me and him," he said. "And even then, he doesn't help much. I usually end up doing most of it. Let me tell you. Those make for some long days."

"I bet they do."

I looked up at Phil as I worked and said, "Dude, get your ass over here and help." K.C. shot me a, *what are you doing?* look, but I continued. "This is a bunch of damn shrimp. The three of us could make quick work of it all. Give us a hand."

Phil took a few steps toward us and applauded, clapping his hands together, deliberate and slow. With a big smile on his face, Phil said, "You guys are doing great. Keep up the good work." Then he leaned back against the big winch.

With the last of the first catch picked through, I was icing down the shrimp while K.C. washed the deck down with the hose. Phil called out, "K.C., get me another cup of coffee."

I looked over at K.C. He shut off the hose and started toward the galley. I stopped him.

"K.C.," I shouted, "That's okay. Go back and finish up what you were doing. I'll get the coffee. I wouldn't mind a cup myself."

Phil smiled and nodded as I walked by, asking, "No cream. No sugar. Right?"

I returned a few minutes later and handed him a fresh cup, ebony black. I took a step or two back and watched as I took a sip from my cup. Phil blew on the hot steaming coffee and took a big sip. He drew the hot liquid into the back of his mouth with a big slurp. I watched with a smile as his facial features pulled in toward his nose. He bent over, shaking his head and spewed coffee all over the deck.

"Goddammit! What the hell was that?"

"You said no cream or sugar, right? What is it? You don't take salt either?" I looked over at K.C., smiled, and winked. "K.C., you take salt in your coffee, don't you?"

K.C. replied with a slight smile and a reluctant nod.

"That's what I thought. Everybody puts a little salt in their Joe. I'm sorry, Mike only has cheap ass table salt. I prefer sea salt."

Phil found nothing funny about my joke, but he wasn't supposed to. He slung the coffee on the deck and threw the cup at me. He was shaking with anger, and wanted to escalate the confrontation, but didn't.

"You son of a bitch. Now clean that up."

My smile was gone now. I picked up his cup off the deck. Phil could tell I too had had about enough. I walked up to him, handed him his cup, and said, "Sure. I'll clean it up. Not a problem. But if you don't like the way I fix your coffee, I suggest you fix your own damn cup."

We locked eyes. I never blinked. Phil turned away in a huff and ducked back into the cabin, slamming the door. K.C. walked up to me and said, "You're really pressing his buttons, Chief."

I turned toward K.C. and put a finger to my lips. *Shhhhhh.*

From the pilot house we could hear Mike holler down, "What in the hell is going on down there?"

Phil shouted, "That smart-ass son of a bitch you brought on board put salt in my coffee, Skip!"

We could hear Skip laugh out loud and say, "Well, next time, maybe you need to pour your own."

Moments later we heard Phil explode again. "Goddammit! You mother... you... Son! Of! A! Bitch!"

"What now, dammit?" asked Mike.

"Skip, the bastard put salt in the pot too!"

Both K.C. and I could hear the smile in Skip's voice. "I don't know what to tell ya, Phil. You best make do. He's only here for the day."

I looked over at K.C. and said, "Shipmate, never fetch him another cup of coffee. You make him get his own. You understand me?"

K.C. nodded with a grin.

K.C. and I culled through two more huge drags.

RED'S RIDE

I 'm an early morning guy and love the sound of quiet and the smell of fresh coastal air. Of all the humans on the Forgotten Coast, I'm one of the few alert enough to enjoy the beginning of each new day. The Navy taught me the benefits of getting up early and getting busy. I get up at 0400 regardless of what might have occurred the night before; it's my running time. If I run low on sleep, I won't pass up an opportunity for a quick midday nap, a little *nooner* as we called it at sea. A sailor must get his rest when he can and get the job done all at the same time. A squid at sea doesn't work your typical corporate nine to five, so a nooner is the perfect remedy.

One morning, I broke my own rules and slept in. I had been running hard, having just returned from a three-day photo shoot at a regatta in St. Petersburg. Between staying out on the water all day, working the evening regatta parties, and the preliminary postproduction work on the pictures, there was little time for rest. I couldn't squeeze a refreshing nooner into the busy schedule.

I rolled into my driveway around midnight. I unloaded my gear and had a generous pour of bourbon to settle my weary body and engaged mind. It was around one in the morning before I crashed. I reached for my alarm. While my internal clock would open my eyes automatically, I always use an alarm as that subtle reminder to get my ass out of bed. I was about to set the alarm when something inside said, *just let it go*. It felt awkward, but I did. I was asleep before my head settled into my pillow.

Like clockwork, my eyes opened at four and I swung my legs out of bed and my feet hit the floor. A creature of habit. After relieving a full bladder, another early morning ritual, I crawled back in bed. Guilt overtook me, but only for a minute or two as I surrendered to what my body was telling me. *Sleep.*

When I went to bed, the sky was crystal clear, full of more stars than most get to see in a lifetime. The darkness of a small coastal town does that. There wasn't any rain in the forecast, so my subconscious found it odd when it absorbed the faint rumble of thunder. I tried to ignore it, but the sound grew and grew until the distant thunder turned to a continuous roar, a roar that seemed to come from the middle of my living room. It startled me out of bed.

Disoriented and confused, I threw on my jeans as the sound fluctuated: Rumble, Rumble, Rumble... Rumble, Rumble, Rumble. "Son of a bitch! What the hell is going on?" I yelled.

I opened the door to my room and dashed into my living room. Lights were flooding the room through my front door glass. I ran over and flung the door open to find the last thing I could have imagined at that time of the morning. It was right there before me, but I still couldn't believe what I was seeing.

There, on my front porch, with its front wheel practically up against the door, was a motorcycle, a Harley Davidson. The rider was vigorously revving the engine, turning the front wheel from one side to another, panning the headlight back and forth. He wore no helmet, only a black skullcap and a smile on his face. The roar of the engine hurt my head and ears. Finally, the rider let the bike go to idle. Then he shut it down.

I could only think of two words. "DAMN, RED!"

In his signature chuckle, Red said, "Morning, sunshine."

My heart was still pounding with excitement and aggravation. "Son of a bitch. Have you lost the keys to your mind? What in the hell do you think you are doing?"

I turned and walked back into the living room, flopped down on the couch and put my face in my hands. I rubbed my eyes to bring some sense of normalcy back into my life. Red followed me in and grabbed a chair. Then he said, "I wanted to come by and see you. I want to talk about..."

Then he paused. He realized something was different, out of place. Then he continued, "Hell. Did I just wake you up? You never sleep this late."

I pulled my fingers down my face as I gazed up at the ceiling in disbelief. Then I looked at him. I said nothing.

"Oh hell, Nigel. I'm sorry. I was just..."

I held up a hand that said, *That's okay. You don't have to explain.* Then I asked, "What time is it, anyway?"

Red looked at the clock on the wall. "Well," he said, chuckling. "Mickey has the big hand on the three and the little hand on the seven."

Damn, I hadn't slept that late in I don't know how long. Ten, twelve years maybe. I felt terrible, worse than when I went to bed. It will probably be another ten or twelve years before I sleep that late again.

"So," I said with a genuine smile. "To what do I owe the pleasure?"

"Well," Red started with a straight face I've rarely experienced, "I wanted to come by and talk to you a bit about something."

"Sounds serious, my friend," I said. "Can I put on some coffee?"

"None for me. I really can't stay too long. But fix a pot for yourself. I know you worship the stuff in the morning. I'll talk while you are a fix'n."

"Sounds like a plan," I said. "And where did the bike come from? I don't remember you having one."

"I've always had it. It's been in storage. That's part of the reason I'm here."

I got up and headed to my small kitchen. "Go on," I said. "I'm listening."

"It's about New Year's, Nigel. I want to talk about New Year's."

That struck me as odd. "Okay," I said. "Hold on a minute." I continued to get the coffee ready. I poured the water in the pot, put the grounds in the filter, and turned the unit on. I walked back to the living room and sat back on the couch. "New Year's?" I asked. "Red, it's a little early for that, isn't it? It's early October. We have months to talk about New Year's."

"Yes, and no," he said. "I'm going to take a little trip. I'm taking off with J.J., my brother. We're going for a ride. We've been planning this for some time."

"A little ride?" I asked. "What do you call a little ride?"

"I don't know. But I doubt I'll be back in time for New Year's."

"So, you're taking off?"

"Yeah, you could say that. My brother and I have some ground to cover and some catching up to do. I haven't seen him in a few years. We need to go."

"I get that, but over three months of riding?" I asked.

"It could be longer. I really don't know."

"What does Trixie have to say about this?"

"She's good with it. She knows I need this."

I said nothing.

"That's why I'm here," he said. "If I'm not back by New Year's, someone will need to manage the fire pit on the beach. That's where you come in."

The New Year's fire pit. It's an annual tradition. In the days leading up to the festivities, Red collects leftover Christmas trees from the streets of Port St. Joe. Once fifteen or so are piled on the trailer, he replants them on the beach to create a small seaside forest. Some are decorated with an assortment of leftover ornaments and celebrated throughout the night. Those undecorated are tossed into the fire pit at midnight to close out the old and bring in the new. It's a special time.

I said nothing and let him talk.

"If it isn't too much to ask, please make sure the fire pit gets dug and the trees are collected and planted. It would make me feel better knowing it was all taken care of. Plus, Trixie can't do it all by herself. She'll need help."

I was a little taken aback. I didn't quite understand what was going on, but I accepted it for what it was, a friend asking a favor. I had plenty of questions, but I figured it best to keep them to myself. No sense in prying.

"Red," I said. "That's not a big deal. You know that. I'd be more than happy to help."

"Good," he said. "I appreciate that." He stood and headed to the door.

I sat there and watched him walk across the floor before I rose to my own feet. "Red? Where are you heading off to now?"

Red turned at the door and said, "I'm going for my ride. My brother is waiting."

I looked beyond Red and toward the street. Resting out on the street was another Harley, its rider sitting in the grass. "Is that your brother?"

"Yes, and he can be a little impatient. He's been waiting a while for this ride, too."

"Well, let me go meet him. I've never had the pleasure."

I headed toward the door when Red gently placed his hand on my chest, stopping me.

"You can't meet him now. It's against the rules. One day later, maybe."

"Don't be ridiculous. Rules? What rules?"

I went to walk past, but Red stopped me again and cast a look that said, *please.*

I stood at the door as Red manhandled his bike back down off the porch. He mounted it and gave the Harley a great kick to start it. His brother did the same. The cacophony of Harley power filled the air for probably five square blocks. I expected to get complaints.

As Red and J.J. rode down the road, I walked out to the mailbox to watch them leave. I could hear them, but I couldn't see much. They were heading east, and the blinding power of the sunrise was more than my eyes could take. In a rumble and a flash, they were gone.

I stood there with squinted eyes and watched the hot fireball as it woke up the sky. I shook my head and smiled. *That crazy Red.* Then I walked back to the house, went inside, and poured a cup of coffee.

I sat down with my coffee, heavy cream, no sugar. I was out of sorts. Waking up so late had me feeling I was running behind. I guess I was. Normally, my coffee maker would be cleaned and put away by now. But here it was, almost 0745, and I was only one cup into a full pot. Chalk it up to experience: Staying in bed doesn't pay off. I can sleep when I'm dead.

My phone bonged. It was an email. I looked at the screen; it was a reminder from my Google calendar. I knew what it was for, but opened the message anyway. *Date night, Candice, 1930 pickup.*

It had been a few weeks since we solved the not-so-clever mystery of Maxine's kidnapping. Luke McKenzie and Maxine were reunited and back to work. Man and goat, happy at last. Those responsible are probably still cleaning out their skivvies. A couple of them shit their pants before it was all over. But in the end, it all concluded well. Life in Port St. Joe was good, almost predictable, but not quite.

It was time to make good on a promise I made to Candice. For her help with Luke and Maxine, I told her we would have dinner one evening. Tonight was the night. I wasn't sure what to expect. She's made no secret about how she feels about me. In the last week alone, I'd received no less than three reports on how she was spreading the word about how things would go. *I'm gonna surprise the shit out of that Nigel Logan. He's not going to know what hit him. He's gonna be blown away.*

I had promised her a nice evening, a dinner, nothing more. I like her as a friend, someone to talk and laugh with. Beyond that, my interest wanes. She is very pretty and sexy, but she's no Barbie doll. She can be a little unpolished, a little rough around the edges, but in an appealing way. She's a little too forward and a little too matter-of-fact, not at all afraid to tell you how she feels. I'm not sure what all she has in mind for the evening, but I hope she isn't disappointed. I'm afraid an evening with Nigel Logan can be quite uneventful. Maybe someone ought to tell her to prepare for boredom. I smiled at the thought.

My phone bonged again. This time a text message. It was short, four words from Candice. *Can't wait until tonight.* I smiled at that too.

After coffee, I went into the spare bedroom, which serves as my little office. I pulled the three memory cards I had stashed away in my camera bag, images from the regatta. I loaded them all in a dedicated folder on the hard drive. There were 1,187 images, all of sailboats, skippers and crew, all working toward a common goal, taking home a pickle platter for the trophy shelf.

Over 1,180 pictures, it sounds like a lot, but not really. It represents over twelve hours of shooting time on the water in perfect conditions. I could have taken thousands more, but I didn't. I'm not a *spray and pray* photographer. I don't fire off five or more frames a second, hoping and praying for a money shot. I like to be selective. I like to think about the image I want, to frame my subject and time the shutter to get the image I'm looking for. I don't always succeed, but I'm getting better at it. Plus, I don't end up with five to six thousand images to sort through in postproduction.

After three hours of deciding which images to keep, dump, or edit, I needed a break. I jumped in the shower to clean up. Then, while standing before the mirror to shave, I took a hard look at myself. *Damn, Logan. You look like a fleabag. Get a freak'n haircut already.*

I walked into Gloria's Salon and Spa on Main Street. The bell mounted at the top of the door frame rang as the door brushed by, an old-school system to alert the owner that another paying customer had walked in the door. It's another example of how this forgotten piece of coastline has stayed frozen in time, where simplicity can rule over many of today's modern advances.

The shop is a small three-bay salon, with stations on the left side, simple privacy curtains extending out between them. On the right were four hair dryers where the gals can sit, read, and gossip while their hairstyles cook. Next to that are two sinks for washing hair. It's a simple, but efficient, setup.

From somewhere within the shop, I heard Gloria say, "Be with you in a sec."

"Take your time," I said as I grabbed an old magazine and took a seat in the little waiting area by the front window. A couple of minutes later, Gloria's head pop out from behind the last curtain where she was working on another patron.

I'm terrible at guessing people's age, but I would put Gloria in her early sixties. She's a little on the heavy side, but not too bad, more like pleasantly plump. She has the most beautiful blue eyes, and they pop against her classic blue rinse and perfectly styled hair. She's a pleasure and always has a kind word.

Gloria flashed me her gorgeous smile and said, "Well, my, my. Now, isn't this something? Look what the cat drug in. Need a trim, do we, dahl'n?"

I smiled back and nodded with a wink.

"Be with you in a minute, sugar. Let me get to a stop'n point with this one here."

I could have gone to the barbershop on Reid Avenue. I probably could have walked in and sat right down, but after twenty-plus years of having my hair cut by old sailors that smell of Old Spice or Aqua Velva, the change of pace was welcomed. Plus, the local intelligence gathered from a salon is more accurate than out of a barbershop. Gals in a salon sort and process information better than a gaggle of old farts sitting around a barbershop playing checkers. If you want to turn a mullet into a 42 inch red fish, go to a barbershop. If you want the juicy details of the truth, go to Gloria's.

I wasn't looking for gossip or information. I needed a haircut, quick and easy, George and Weezy.

I looked up from my magazine to see Gloria's hand extended toward me. "Come on, sweetie, let's wash that mop first." I got up, and she led me to the first sink. I sat down and put my head back into the basin as she placed a towel around my neck. She wet my hair, applied some apple-scented shampoo, and went to scrubbing my head as she talked.

"So, what brings you in today?" she said as her fingers aggressively worked the lather into my brain.

"Having dinner with a friend tonight, so I want to knock off the rough edges. Get a trim," I said.

"A friend, well, anybody I know?" she asked with a hint of heightened awareness.

I said nothing at first. The question was asked with too much deliberate inflection. She already knew something before I even sat down and wasn't looking for an answer. She was looking for confirmation. That didn't surprise me.

"Now, Gloria. Are you going to stand there and pretend that..."

From across the room, a loud, forceful, slightly panicked, but familiar, voice called out from behind the last curtain. "Who's out there? Gloria, who are you talking to?"

"No one, dear," said Gloria. "Sit tight. I'll be with you in a minute."

"Don't feed me that. I heard you. Who are you talking to?"

"Candice?" I asked. "Is that you?"

Gloria giggled as she rinsed.

"Nigel Logan! Are you out there?" She turned in her chair to look. "Oh, shit! What in the hell are you doing here?"

"I'm here to get a..."

"Get out, dammit. Get out of here right now. Son of a bitch! I can't freak'n believe this."

I lifted my head and craned to the right to look. It was the wrong thing to do. There was Candice, not looking her best. Her hair was going in every direction, flat panels of aluminum foil everywhere, ready to tune in alien radio transmissions. Plus, she had green goop on her face, some cosmetic mask. I got lambasted.

"DO NOT LOOK AT ME! Turn your head, now. Oh my God! I can't believe this is happening."

Candice went on and on. I looked at Gloria with a hint of a smile as I shook my head. "You are so bad," I said low enough that only she could hear.

"Are you still here? I told you to leave. O! M! G!"

"Okay! Okay! I'm leaving already," I said.

Gloria did her best to towel off my wet head as I walked across the floor. When I got to the door, I tried to pay for the scrub, but Gloria shook her head with a smile and said, "No charge, sweetie. I should pay you. That was priceless."

I kissed Gloria on the cheek and opened the door. The bell rang. I stopped in the doorway and turned. "See you at 7:30. Be ready. I'm never late."

There was silence.

"Candice? Did you hear me?"

"GET OUT!"

"Okay. See ya then."

I walked out onto the sidewalk, my head still soaking wet. I turned left and went around the corner. Two minutes later, I was sitting in a chair, looking out a window, watching the red and blue spiral of a barber's pole move upwards. As I listened to the sound of scissors clipping, the smell of Brut aftershave was all around my head. I smiled.

At 1925 I was sitting in the driveway of Candice's house. I'm always on time, or at least try to be. At 1930, I walked up to knock on the door, but as I was about to knuckle up, it flew open. Candice stood there for a moment and glared at me, then brushed by. She didn't even offer a hello. She stormed by, walked out, and got in my truck. *Games. I don't do games well.*

I stood at the door and didn't budge, stood there looking at her. I waited. She sat there, looking straight ahead, not at me, but straight ahead. I continued to wait, then I waited some more.

After several minutes, she got out of the truck and stormed back to the porch. "Well?" she said.

"Get back in the house."

"What?"

"I said get back in the house and maybe we'll try this again."

She said nothing. She huffed and went back inside.

I waited a good two minutes and knocked on the door. It flew open. She looked indignant, with a hint of embarrassment, a strange combination. It softened when I smiled. I took her in with my eyes. I said nothing. She couldn't stand the silence any longer and asked, "What? What is it?"

"You look great," I said. "Really. You look fantastic."

I meant it, every word. Her hair was gorgeous, time well spent at Gloria's. She was sporting a color I like on her, a hazelnut with blond highlights. The same color she wore when she helped me out a few weeks ago, tearing down the "Wanted" posters that Luke McKenzie put up all over town. She was in weathered jeans and a white blouse that partially showed through a black leather jacket that perfectly matched her cowboy boots. Everything she had on perfectly showcased all her best features.

Her look softened some more into a genuine smile. "Thank you, Nigel. I'm sorry for acting the way I did earlier."

"I don't know what you are talking about," I said. "Are you ready?"

We pulled out of the drive and headed toward Highway 98. Her perfume was an immense improvement over the normal smell of my truck, usually a combination of stale beer and french fries. The pine-tree-shaped air freshener that hangs from the rearview mirror always struggles to stay ahead of the stench.

A victim of her occupation, she normally smells worse than my truck, of beer and cigarette smoke. You would expect that, I guess, from anybody that makes a living working a small bar in a town with no smoking ordinances. Tonight, however, all of that was washed away and what she had on was a delicate floral scent, not overbearing, pleasant to the nose. My nose anyway. I liked it.

I came to the first stop sign, slowed, then stood on the brakes, enough to cause a slight lunge forward. I looked in my rearview to check for oncoming traffic. There was none. "So," I said. "Where to? What do you have a hankering for?"

"Really?" she asked. "I get to pick? Most guys just head straight to some bar with food and a big TV."

"I don't know if you've noticed, but I'm not from around here. And you know, come to think of it, this is my first night out with anyone since I came to town. Maybe I'm not in tune with local protocol, but where I come from, the lady gets to pick."

"No one's called me a lady before."

I said nothing at first. I took my time and drove on through the intersection. "Just think about it and let me know. Any place you please."

"Can we hear some music?" she asked. Without waiting for an answer, she reached over and turned on the radio. She was adjusting the volume. "Is that too loud?"

I shook my head. "That's fine."

Through the speakers, Oyster Radio filled the truck cab with rhythm and melody. It was "Salt in the Blood," written and performed by our local friend, Brian Bowen. It's a great tune celebrating the life and times of local watermen. It's a favorite, but unfortunately, we missed most of it. It was just going off.

Candice said, "Dang. I love that song."

"Me too. He's playing at the Raw Bar tonight. We could ride out there after dinner."

"Let's go now. For dinner."

"You want the Raw Bar for dinner?" I asked, sounding surprised.

"Is there a problem with that?"

"Absolutely not, I thought that... that you might want something more sit down, more white tablecloth... more quiet. Italian or something."

The look on her face politely told me to shut up, so I did. Then she used some of my own words and threw them back at me. "I don't know if you've noticed, but I *am* from around here. I'm not Italian. I'm local. Local and proud of what my area offers. That's the protocol around here." She smiled and continued, "Plus, having Brian playing on the porch and sharing some baked oysters with you sounds nice enough for me."

I said nothing. I turned the truck around and headed out Highway 98 toward Indian Pass. As I drove, she listened to the radio, and I got to thinking. *The Raw Bar has food, plenty of big television sets, and even more beer.* Then I asked her a question. "Candice. Tell me something. If you were going out with some other fella from around here, where would he have taken you?"

"Probably the Raw Bar."

Then I said, "Well, I don't get it. What's the point? Why would you make such a big deal about getting to pick where we went?"

She slid over and kissed me on the cheek. "It isn't about where we go. It's about you letting me pick where to go. I never get to pick. It was nice knowing I had options."

She slid back to her side of the truck and smiled. I drove on in silence, glancing over at her from time to time. She is always attractive, but on that night, she was beautiful.

The Raw Bar was crowded for early October. We ended up parking out on the highway and walking, not at all unusual. As we got out of the car, we could hear Brian's music over the normal ruckus of the porch crowd. He acknowledged us with a singing smile and a nod as we came onto the porch.

The Forgotten Coast Shrimp and Oyster Bar, or Raw Bar, as it's more commonly known, is one of the true local establishments; it's where people meet. When you first arrive, it is hand-shaking and *howdy, glad to see ya* all across the porch. Candice grabbed my arm and said, "I will run inside and get our names on the list to eat. Can I get you a beer?"

"That sounds like a magnificent idea. Thanks." She gave me a smile and my arm a little extra squeeze before turning to head for the door. I looked up to see Trixie, Red's wife, walking toward me. I met her halfway with a kiss and a hug.

"Fill me in, Trix," I said. "What is going on with Red? What's with this ride?"

"There isn't much to tell," she said. "His brother showed up at the house this morning and said, 'Let's go!' They haven't seen each other in a few years, so Red packed his saddlebags and took off."

"Just like that?"

"Just like that."

I said nothing.

Trixie continued, "Red said he was tired, that he needed to reconnect with nature, and that a ride would be good therapy. Like a Henry David Thoreau walkabout, but on a motorcycle. Plus, he would get to spend time with his brother. He has missed him so."

"How long do you expect he'll be gone?"

Trixie smiled and lit a cigarette. She took a draw and exhaled. She laughed and said, "With that crazy Red of mine. Who the hell knows?" Then she turned and walked away, catching Brian between songs. "Play some of that Jack Johnson, dammit!"

He did.

The list of folks waiting to eat wasn't that long. Candice and I shared an order of baked Apalachicola oysters and steamed shrimp. They were fabulous, as usual. We had a good time. I shared stories from my Navy days, and she told me much about her previous marriages and worthless husbands. The entertainment value was very high, and we did a lot of laughing. That was nice. I hadn't laughed like that since before my troubles back in Norfolk. It felt good.

After dinner, we headed back out onto the porch to mingle and listen to Brian. It was a beautiful night. The sky was clear, which meant every star was visible to the naked eye. The moon was enormous, not full, but plenty big to cast great illumination down on the earth. There isn't much in the way of ground lighting out on the Pass to interfere with stargazing.

A light breeze worked its way through the trees. That told me it was probably blowing eight to ten knots out on the bay, perfect conditions for an evening sail. It was a gorgeous evening.

I looked across the porch and saw Candice hanging out in the parking lot with old friends, mostly guys, probably from her high school days. She was sitting on the back of an opened tailgate, her boots swinging in the air. They were laughing, having a good time. I kept my eye on her until she caught me looking at her. She smiled. I motioned for her to come and she jumped from the truck and walked toward me. All the guys watched her as she headed my way. There was no doubt about it; the girl knows how to walk.

"Have you ever been sailing?" I asked.

"I went out on one of those catamaran things once. It turned over, wasn't fun. A fishing boat had to stop and help us."

"That's not sailing," I said. "Well... it is, but not the kind of sailing I'm talking about."

I looked toward the stars and sky, then toward the trees. I turned back and said, "I got a text message from my boat. She wants to get underway. Are you interested? It should be a nice sail." She gave me a grin that told me everything I needed to know. *Let's go.*

In less than forty-five minutes, we were motoring out of the channel and into the bay. Ten minutes later, the motor was off, and we were sailing. I didn't want to work too hard, so I hoisted the full mainsail and the smaller working jib. Normally, I would carry a much larger headsail, but for a simple midnight cruise, this would be perfect.

I set a course that took us out of St. Joe Bay and into the Gulf of Mexico. The boat was on a close reach and moving well. I set the autopilot. We would be on this heading for a while before clearing the point and falling off a few points toward deeper water.

I excused myself and made my rounds about the boat, both on deck and down below. I knew everything was secure, but as a creature of habit, I always take another look once underway. As expected, everything was fine. I returned to the cockpit to find Candice sitting to leeward, the low side, her hand reaching for the water. The occasional swell would dip her fingers into the salty seawater.

"Wine?" I asked. "A glass of red sounds nice."

"And a blanket, maybe?" she replied.

We were enjoying an effortless sail down the coast. Soft music filled the cockpit. I shut down the autopilot to steer by hand, my favorite. Without a doubt, we were a visual treat for anyone onshore paying attention. With the moon reflecting off *MisChief's* clean, white sails, there would be no missing us. It was perfect.

We enjoyed the sail with little conversation. I think even Candice picked up on the fact that too much talk could ruin the experience. That it would interfere with the mood of the boat.

On a sailboat, a skipper does a lot more listening than talking. Not listening, as in listening to other people, but listening, as in listening to the boat. A sailboat will tell you everything you need to know, if you know what you're hearing.

The breeze picked up a bit and the old girl responded, putting her chin in the swells and surging down the coast. She met each wave with the grace only an old full-keeled boat can offer. It was a smooth and easy motion. Everybody was happy. The boat, the passenger, and the Skipper were all in a good place.

We sailed for a full hour and a half before tacking the boat to head back toward the cape. The commotion of the sails, first luffing, and then filling again after crossing over the deck of the boat, got Candice's attention. She looked at me inquisitively.

"Heading back," I said.

She nodded in confirmation before asking, "More wine?"

"No thanks. I've had enough for now. But pour yourself another glass."

She went below and came back with her glass fully charged. She again settled on the leeward side of the cockpit, closest to the water. She took a sip, then looked at me and mouthed the words, *Thank you*. I smiled back with a wink.

The sail back was great, perfect therapy for a guy that needed some slow-time in his life. As usual, the boat was well behaved. She practically sailed herself, a light touch on the tiller. *Slow-time*. That was how best to describe the night with Candice, *slow-time*.

It had been a perfect night, different from what I had expected. Nowhere was the normally aggressive, sassy, flirtatiously-forward Candice to be found. I looked at her as she cuddled up underneath the blanket in the corner of the cockpit, both hands cradling her glass of wine, her back resting against the doghouse cabin. She struck me as someone I had never met before, a stranger. A beautiful stranger, someone I might want to get to know better. I smiled and laughed to myself. *Look at yourself, Logan. You would have never thought in a million years that you would see her as you see her right now.* Candice caught me with a huge smile on my face.

"What is it?" she sat up slightly and asked, "Why the big grin?"

Slightly embarrassed, I said, "Ah, nothing. I enjoy sailing my boat, that's all." She went back to her casual posture. Then I recalled something I heard before our date. Candice had told a few folks she was going to blow me away. I guess she did.

I entered the channel, into the protected waters of the bay. Then headed toward a small cove just inside the point of the cape and brought the boat head to wind. *MisChief's* momentum kept her moving forward, straight into the wind.

"What's happening?" Candice asked. "What are we doing?"

"Dropping a hook. It's too pretty to head in yet," I said, dropping the headsail to the deck. I turned toward her. "That is... if it's alright? I mean, if you want to go back in..."

She interrupted me with a grin and a shake of the head. I went back to dropping canvas. The boat was still moving forward with an easy motion, tracking straight. I casually went forward and deployed my anchor and about 50 feet of chain.

With the sails all stowed and everything put in order, it was time to slow down even more. I jumped into the cockpit. "That's better," I said with a smile. "I'll take that glass of wine now."

Candice jumped up and said, "Well, let me be a good barkeep and pour that for you, sir."

She went below and I looked around the deck. Something was missing. I glanced all around and finally looked up the rig toward the sky. I saw the sun's bright reflection bouncing off Venus. It was beautiful, but it wasn't the light I expected to see.

I called down to Candice, "If you please. The electrical panel to star-board, on the right side of the boat, you'll find a switch labeled *anchor*. Throw it, please."

Three seconds later, the masthead was aglow with white light, 360 degrees around, visible for miles. Five seconds after that, Candice came up with our wine. She sat next to me and grabbed the blanket so we could share, covering our legs. She sat close. I didn't mind, and the wine was good.

We sat back and enjoyed the spectacular, clear evening and each other's company. It's tough to be on a boat, with a night so clear, stars shining bright, and not ultimately talk about it.

Candice knew little about celestial bodies, which was fine. A navigator by trade, it gave me plenty to talk about. She knew the Big Dipper, but I guess most everyone does. It must be the most recognizable constellation in the northern hemisphere; much the way the Southern Cross is below the equator.

I told her, "Follow the seven stars of the Big Dipper, starting with the first star of the handle. Stop with the sixth star and study the distance between the sixth and seventh star."

"Okay," she said. "Got it."

"Now follow onto the seventh star, but keep going in the same direc-tion for about five times the length of the distance between the sixth and seventh star. You should see a small star, sitting by its lonesome."

I gave her a few moments to study the sky before asking, "Do you see it? It's right there," I said, trying to help by pointing a finger.

"Yes," she said. "I think so. That little star there?" She pointed with me.

"Yup! That one."

"What about it? Looks pretty insignificant."

"Not really," I said. "Congratulations. You located Polaris."

"Really? That little star has a name?"

"Yup, but most refer to it as the North Star."

"That's the North Star?" she said in astonishment. "That little thing?"

"Yup!" I said. "That little thing. Not exactly insignificant, huh?"

We continued to have wine and conversation until the bottles were empty and the chatter used up. We reduced ourselves to enjoying the silence underneath the stars. A deeper chill set in and I got us another blanket. Between the two blankets and our shared body heat, we were plenty warm. The quiet continued and Candice took more of a snuggling posture. I put my arm around her and allowed her to settle in. She was asleep in no time.

I looked down at her and smiled, laughed inside. *Expect the unexpected.* I was happy things worked out the way they did, and I tilted my head back and found Venus, still the brightest thing in the sky. I closed my eyes.

Startled, my eyes flew open and my heart skipped a beat. The sound of thunder got my immediate attention. I looked around. Candice was still asleep. I heard it again. It made no sense. The sky was as we left it, perfectly clear. I heard it again. Then I realized... it wasn't thunder. It was the same muffler roar that woke me up earlier that morning. Yes, that's exactly what it sounded like, but made no sense, not out in the middle of the bay. I looked toward the sky and found shooting stars, two of them. They were flying across the heavens, one bright white, the other a fiery red. I watched as they stretched across the black, starry sky until they disappeared over the horizon.

I smiled and said, "Love you, brother."

I looked down at Candice, pulled her in closer, and shut my eyes.

THIRTEEN

I was hungry. A half-eaten Subway sandwich from the day before sat in the fridge. Perfect. It was a little soggy from the oil and vinegar, but it was tasty and hit the spot. The only improvement would have been a generous splash of Crystal Hot Sauce, but I found my only bottle almost empty. There was just enough in the bottle's bottom to piss you off. I stood there, trying to shake whatever was left out of the bottle. *Dribble... Dribble.* "Crap!"

I stood in the express checkout line behind a couple of tourists at the Piggly Wiggly. Miss Marge was behind the register. I had three bottles of Crystal in my hand. Marge saw me in line and offered a private wink.

Marge is my next-door neighbor. She keeps an eye on my place while I'm out of town. We never discuss it, but I keep an eye out for her place, too. She's a sweet, single gal, a retired widow, comfortable in her skin and where she is in life. A great combination.

"Three bottles? Really? That's all you need?" Marge asked, as she scanned the items.

"Yep. That'll do for now," I said. "I needed some twenty minutes ago, but I was out. Hate it when that happens."

"Hey," Marge added, "that Candice girl came by to see you yesterday. You were gone, or I assumed you were. Your truck wasn't in the drive."

"It mustn't have been too important," I said. "She didn't call."

"I don't know. She sat in her car for a while then went to knock at the back door."

I said nothing. *Wonder what she wanted?*

"She really likes you; you know?"

"She's a great friend," I said, smiling. "I'm quite fond of her."

"As fond of her as she is of you?"

"Come on now, Marge. Give me a break. You're as bad as the gals at Miss Gloria's." Miss Gloria's parlor is the hotbed of local intelligence and personal beauty.

"Well, I do get my hair done there."

"Okay, I got to run. Besides, you have folks waiting to check out."

Marge took one last shot. "I'm jus' say'n, Nigel. You can't ignore the obvious."

I headed toward the door and said, "Love you too, Marge." The doors slid open and closed behind me as I walked out into the warmth of the sunshine.

I took a right out of the parking lot and drive down to Jetty Park, do a fly-by and see what was going on, cruise through and check out the license tags. I like to see where folks are visiting from.

The lot was almost full. Many of the usual suspects were there, the locals that like to fish the jetty rocks. I also saw plates from Wisconsin, Ontario, and even one from Montana. Man, *you're a long way from home.* I lifted my head and looked toward the fishing pier. It isn't big, like those that stretch way out over the water. It pokes out a few feet over the seawall.

A crowd had gathered on the pier. They were watching some goings-on over the side. That usually means someone has hooked into something good. But they weren't looking out over the water. They focused on the rocks behind the seawall.

Curiosity got the best of me. I got out of my truck.

Indeed, someone had caught a big fish, a shark. It was about a five to five-and-a-half-foot reef shark. Someone had hooked it, but how it made it over the seawall and into the shallow tidal pool was a mystery.

I assessed the situation. There was a guy with the fish, trying to return it to the bay. He was limited in size and strength, but that didn't keep him from staying with it. He was working alone despite an ample supply of able-bodied men that were watching from the pier. They were content to be bystanders while this great fish was about to die. *Pussies, every one of them.*

I immediately made my way down the rocks toward the pool and fish. I looked up toward the pier and said to no particular person, "It's just a fish, not like a rabid dog, dammit. It won't bite you out of spite. For Christ's sake, is nobody going to help this guy?"

Nobody replied, probably out of embarrassment. I did, though, catch the attention of the rescuer. "Thanks, mate," he said in the Queen's English. "Be careful. The rocks are slick, yeah? Sharp oyster shells, too."

"Got it."

"Bloody hell. You're in flops."

"I know. Not ideal."

He had the fish by the tail and was standing up on the seawall. The shark's face was down in the warm, stagnant, dark pool of water. "I can't get her over. She's too heavy, yeah? She'll drown soon if we can't get her back."

I said nothing and entered the pool. Two careful steps in and my right foot slipped off its flip-flop. An oyster shell or sharp rock dug into the bottom of my right foot. "Son of a bitch!" I said.

"Be careful," said the guy holding the tail.

I clenched my teeth, thinking only of the infection that was most certainly going to set in. I also decided the stability of my bare feet would serve me better, so I reached down and took off my flops. Still aggravated by the lack of help from the photo and video paparazzi, I threw each flop like a tomahawk at the crowd. "Here! Somebody make yourself useful and hold these for me." They ducked and dodged as the projectiles whizzed by their heads.

I made my way down to the shark, slipping here and there. I rubbed its head and dorsal. It turned an eye toward me and seemed to look right through me. "Easy girl. Easy. Everything is going to be alright." I looked up at the guy with the tail and asked, "How long has she been out of the water?"

"I don't know," he said, "a while. It seems like forever."

I continued to pet the fish. "We need to hurry then."

"How do you want to do this?" he asked.

"Straight away. If you can lift the tail a bit and give me some room to grab under her belly, I'm going to reach around her, right behind her dorsal and pectoral fins, put her in a bear hug and pick her up."

I was getting into a better position when I heard a voice from the pier. "You better be careful, Nigel Logan. Please."

I looked up and found Candice. She wasn't smiling, her eyes full of concern, framed by a new hair color, strawberry blond. It looked great on her. Seeing her brought a bit of levity to the situation. She was a welcomed distraction that lightened the mood. I smiled back and added a wink.

"Who is that?" My new friend asked.

"A friend."

"A smok'n hot friend, yeah?"

I agreed, but ignored the comment. "Come on, let's get on with this."

With my left hand, I reached around and grabbed behind the dorsal and took hold underneath the left pectoral fin. The shark twisted, not as a threat, but to let us know she was ready for this to be over too. I said, "If you can lift and twist her to the left a bit. I can get underneath her."

He didn't have to. As if she understood what I needed, the shark went nose down in the tidal pool, arched her back up, and tilted to the left. I didn't hesitate. I saw my opportunity and quickly got my right hand and arm under her torso. I gave her a firm squeeze and lifted. She didn't protest.

There was no way I could have stepped up on the seawall. It was too high, and she was too heavy, so I took a couple of careful steps and lifted her on top of the wall, right at the feet of the Brit. I looked up at him and we both smiled. I petted the fish one last time, then gave her a healthy shove. "Now, get your ass back where you belong," I said as the fish went over the side.

At first, it didn't look good. The great fish quickly rolled onto her back. She stayed there for what seemed an eternity. I crawled up on the seawall for a better view. We watched and waited. I was holding my breath, watching. I exhaled in relief when she moved from side to side and rolled right-side up. We watched as the shark, tired and fatigued, took her time swimming for deeper water.

A hand patted me on the back. I turned to see a hand being offered in my direction. I took it. "Thanks, mate," said the Brit. "The name is Pete Billingsly."

"Pleasure's mine, Pete. I'm Nigel. Nigel Logan."

"I already knew that, yeah? Your girlfriend introduced you earlier, remember?"

"Well, she really isn't my girlfriend. Just a real good friend."

I looked up and found her waiting at the top of the rocks. She had my flip-flops in one hand and a huge smile on her face. She blew me a kiss and motioned with her finger for me to come. I smiled back.

"That's more than a real good friend, mate. Don't feed me your rubbish. She fancies you. That's clear."

Pete tapped me on the arm and pointed down at the pool of blood I was standing in. The bottom of my right foot was leaking a steady stream of red stuff all over the seawall, running into the bay. "You've got to get that taken care of, spit spot."

I nodded in agreement. I look up and called, "Candice. Go get my truck and bring it around, please. I'm hurt and you'll need to drive."

Pete helped me up and across the rocks to where Candice was waiting. Together, they helped me to the truck. I didn't really need that much attention, but I didn't complain. With my foot wrapped in a towel, I shook Pete's hand from out the passenger side window and thanked him. Then I turned toward Candice. "Get me home, please."

"You need a doctor. You're going to the emergency room."

"Not yet. I can wait to be seen. Got to clean this thing out now before the crud sets in. Then we'll go, if it's necessary. A lot of blood doesn't mean a lot of wound."

We got back to my place, and Candice ran hot water in the tub. I sat on the edge and held my foot as I tried to figure out the best way to get the cut into the stream of water. Turns out there isn't a good way for a right-handed person to handle a wound on the bottom of their right foot, so I stuck my heel into the stream of hot water.

The second the water hit the cut, I clenched my teeth and sucked all the air out of the room. *Shit! That hurts.* But I knew the hurting had just begun. It would have to be scrubbed out. I looked at Candice. The anguish on her face spoke volumes. I smiled and said, "It's going to be alright. Can you see it? Tell me, how bad is it?"

She leaned over and took my foot, tilted it so she could see. "Pretty bad. A gash. Maybe two inches long."

"Shit! Probably from an oyster shell. How deep?"

"Hard to say."

"Squeeze it open and take a peep."

She did and gasped.

"That bad, huh?"

"I'm afraid so."

"Well, okay then," I said. "Let's get this thing scrubbed and head to the ER."

I got into the tub on my knees so Candice could get the cut open and let the stream of hot water enter deep inside. The water flush was painful, but necessary. I directed Candice to a soft brush and antibacterial soap. "Open it up and scrub it out good," I told her. "Go at it angry like. Like it's your first husband or something."

Candice said, "They're going to do this at the ER, anyway. So why not let them do it?"

"Because the bacteria that harbors in stagnant pools are aggressive. I want a head start on any infection, especially if I end up having to wait two hours in the ER waiting room."

She didn't say another word, but went right to it. The brush and the sting of the soap felt like she was raking it out with a wire brush. I growled, saying, "It seems... Damn, that hurts... Like you might enjoy this a little too much."

She stopped scrubbing and put the cut back into the water to rinse. I gritted my teeth and winced as I listened. "I would enjoy this more if you were Phil."

"Phil? Who's Phil?"

"Phil Stewart. He was my first husband."

"Your first husband?"

"Uh huh."

"Phil Stewart? As in the Phil Stewart that works for Mike Bobo on the shrimp boat?"

"Yep. One and the same. Piece of work. But I guess you already know that, huh?"

"Does he know who I am?"

"Oh, yeah. He knows. You're not a favorite."

That explained a lot. I met Phil the week before, when I volunteered to help Mike on his boat. He was short-handed, and while I knew nothing about shrimp'n, I'm no stranger to boats. I pick up easily, and a quick-learning hand beats no hand at all.

From the second I stepped aboard; this Phil guy treated me like crap. He didn't appreciate having an extra body, and he certainly didn't want me on board. Now it made sense.

"I came by to see you yesterday, to warn you," said Candice. "I left a note on the door, but I never heard from you."

"Warn me about what?"

"Phil was in the bar a couple of nights ago. He had been drinking pretty heavy, which he always does. He was spouting off to his friends about wanting to kick your ass. That the next time he saw you, you had better watch out."

"What in the hell is his beef with me, dammit?"

"Me," Candice said. "He's very jealous and can't stand the idea I could go out with anyone else."

"And this was your first husband? I don't need this kind of shit, Candice."

"I know. I'm sorry. I thought I should tell you. Are you worried?"

"About Phil? No, not particularly. Should I be?"

"Well, he can be like a bulldog. Doesn't want to let go of things. So, I guess what I'm saying is, you can probably expect trouble at some point, especially if he's been drinking."

Wonderful. I sat up and thought about it while my foot continued to throb and said, "Perhaps you should have Phil talk to your last husband."

Candice said, "I don't think that would do any good."

"Why's that?"

"Because Phil used to beat up Billy pretty regularly. At least while we were married."

I laughed at that. *What a tough guy.*

Before heading to the hospital, I checked my selection of bourbon and pulled out a bottle of Four Roses, their single barrel. I drew myself a generous, neat, four-finger long pour in an old-fashioned glass before we walked out the door. Good 100 proof. I wanted it in my system before they started driving that Novocaine needle in the bottom of my foot.

We stayed in the parking lot until I could finish my drink. I was calm about the entire ordeal, but the drink polished off my demeanor to a bright, carefree shine. I wasn't drunk much, but enjoyed a quiet glow. I looked down at my cocktail glass. It was empty. I could have used one more swallow... *Damn.*

I was looking through the windshield at the emergency room entrance when Candice leaned over toward me and gave me a long kiss on my cheek. I turned toward her and realized my brain and tongue were not fully in sync. I was more comfortably numb than I thought. "What was that for?" I said with a small smile.

"It was for me, if I have to be honest," she said.

"I love honesty!" I said with a slight slur. "Always be honest... with me, always. I'll appreciate that."

"Have dinner with me tonight?" She said with a slight grin.

I slowly squinted and closed my right eye. I see better in close quarters with my left. I wanted to see her clearly. "Are you trying to take advantage of me? Catch me in a weak moment?" I asked in a jovial, suspicious tone.

"Well," she said with a smile. "Maybe I am."

"More honesty! I love it!"

"Well?"

"You're on. It's the least I can do. I owe you big for coming through and taking care of me one more time."

She turned away. The smile on her face retreated to a thin, straight line, and her eyes were saturated with disappointment. I watched her carefully before asking, "Is there something wrong?"

"No, I guess not."

"Candice," I said with my right eye still closed. "Don't give me any of that. What's wrong? Honesty, remember?"

She turned back toward me. "Okay, then." She paused for a moment and said, "I was hoping you might have dinner with me because you'd like to spend time with me, not because of some obligation to repay a debt."

That stung. I hurt her. *Dammit.* There was no way of trying to dance around what I said. It was already out there. She turned to look at me after I tugged on her hand. "I'm an idiot. I'm sorry. Please forgive me."

She said nothing.

"Candice," I said, doing my best to sound coherent. "I've been drinking, so I think the less I say, the better. I already have to pull this size thirteen out of my throat." That made her smile. I continued, doing my best not to slur my words too much. "Listen... I enjoy your company very much. There's a lot I am sorting out personally. Please be patient with me. Okay?"

She still said nothing, but nodded her head with a grin.

We got out of the car and headed toward the emergency room door. I reached down and grabbed her hand as we walked. She was strolling. I was limping along on the ball of my right foot. The sliding glass door opened up and a wall of cool air rushed out and hit us in the face when she asked, "A size thirteen, huh? Really?"

"What?" I said with a slight shiver.

"Thirteen. Your shoe size. You know what they say about a man and the size of his..."

"Candice! For crying out loud."

She giggled as we walked up to the reception window. The girl helping us behind the window was Karen. It said so, right on her name tag. She looked up and said, "Hey, Candice." *An old schoolmate, perhaps.* "Who is this? What can we do for y'all?"

Again, I spoke carefully. "My name is Nigel Logan. I have a pretty deep oyster shell cut on the bottom of my right foot."

Candice leaned over in front of me and told Karen with great emphasis and a wink, "It's a size thirteen."

I stood there, half in shock, half embarrassed. Karen looked me over, smiled and said, "Lucky girl, you."

Oh, brother!

THE CARD

R ed and I sat at the Raw Bar when this fella takes a seat next to Red. It was obvious the guy was a newbie, so Red gave him the rundown, which was met with the standard reaction of amazement. *Really? Get my own beers, keep track of what I eat and drink, then pay before I leave? Really?*

As the guy got up to head to the cooler, I noticed he was wearing a North Sails ball cap and a regatta t-shirt from the 2013 MC Scow Nationals. A fellow racing sailor, I don't run across too many of those here on the Forgotten Coast. Fishing rules the waters here. There are a few sailboats in Port St. Joe, but the sailing scene is mostly local cruisers and transients passing through to other destinations. There is no active racing being campaigned here.

The MC Scow is a great one-design racing boat. It is most often singlehanded, although it can be doublehanded as well. It is sixteen-foot long with a very flat hull shape and wide bow, like a big surfboard with a single sail, a huge mainsail. In a blow, an MC can be a challenge, but they are fast and exciting. It's a very popular class.

Once the stranger settled back at the bar, I leaned forward, looking past Red and said, "Love me some MC Scows. How did you do at Nationals?" nodding toward his shirt.

The stranger said, "Oh, thanks. Been sailing the MC for over ten years now. Love it. Do you sail one too?"

"I've borrowed one from time to time. An OPB is my favorite boat to race."

Red looked over at me, interrupting. "OPB?"

"I'm sorry, Red. OPB. Other People's Boat."

Red mumbled, "Cheap bastard," and took a sip from his beer.

I reached across in front of Red and offered my hand to the stranger, "Nigel Logan, here. And this is my very non-sailing buddy, Red."

The guy met me halfway, and we shook hands. "I'm Bradley, Bradley Cain. Pleased to meet you." Then he shook Red's hand.

"You didn't answer me," I said. "How did you do at Nationals?"

"I didn't," replied Cain. "I was on race committee. My club hosted the event, and I volunteered to be PRO." *PRO, Primary Race Officer.*

"Ah. That's too bad," I said.

"Not really. It's an honor to oversee a national event that puts over sixty boats on the line. I get a big kick out of running the show, almost as much as racing and finishing middle of the pack."

"I know what you mean," I said. "I'm a regatta photographer, and as much as I like to sail, I never tire of grabbing images of boats." I took a sip of my beer and motioned for another dozen raw oysters before asking, "Where are you from, Bradley?"

"I live in Flowery Branch, Georgia and sail out of the Lanier Sailing Club, but I'm coming off a regatta in Pensacola and passing through to Lake Eustis. The class has a regional event down there next weekend."

I laughed, looking down at my oysters as they were being delivered, and said, "Well, you just answered my next question. I'll be at Lake Eustis too. I'm shooting the event, so I guess I'll be seeing you down there."

"Perfect!" he said. "Keep an eye out for sail number 2035. Do you have a card?"

I got out my wallet and pulled out a stack of business cards and flipped through them. "Hold on now," I said aloud. "I know I have a few in here somewhere."

I riffled through the stack of cards, dealing them out on the bar as I reviewed each one: insurance card, my Navy Federal account card, a Freedom Bonds and Bails card, one of Red's driving school cards, my Navy Shellback card, and business cards from other various nautical photographers I've met along the way. *It's no wonder my wallet is so damn fat.*

Then I came across a card that made me pause. I hadn't thought of or seen that card in a very long time. I flipped it over and stared at the back. The phone number was there, just as I remembered it.

I'm not sure how long I sat there staring at the card, but Red said, "Hey! Earth to Logan. Did you forget what you were doing? You're getting the man a business card, for crying out loud."

I looked up, half startled, "Huh? Oh... Yeah. I'm sorry."

I zipped through the other cards until I found one of my own. There were three. I took out two and handed them to Mr. Cain. "Here ya go. Sorry 'bout that. Got a tad bit distracted."

I collected my cards and sorted them into two stacks, one for keeping and one for the shit can. I placed the others back in my wallet but left the one card out. It brought back vivid memories: stress, anxiety, and consequences, mainly my premature retirement from the world's most powerful Navy.

I stared at the card as it took me back to the day it was handed to me. I heard her words as if it were yesterday. *When you're ready.*

It was a little after 1500 when my cell phone rang. It woke me up. I didn't know how long I'd been asleep, maybe three, three and a half hours. The TV was on. The last thing I remembered was filtering through the noon news, keeping an ear out for anything of interest.

The local television stations were following the case very close. It even got some mild attention from some of the national news outlets. Emotions were on high alert, and the circumstances created great conflict and debate amongst all the local legal analysts. If something new were to develop, they would interrupt normal broadcasting to announce the latest. All of Norfolk, VA, wanted to know, but no one more than me.

I picked up the cell phone. "This is Logan."

I remained on my back, looking at the ceiling as I listened. The caller didn't take long. The message was short.

I ended the call, tossing the phone to the foot of the bed.

I laced my fingers together, placed my hands behind my head, and settled back into my pillow. My eyes found a small spider crawling across the ceiling. I followed it toward the wall and watched as it fell, a fine thread of silk controlling its descent. It landed on the lampshade. It was free, self-reliant, bothering nobody.

I rolled over, grabbed the remote, turned up the TV, threw my legs over the side, and put my feet on the floor. I stretched. Then I walked into the full kitchen, a nice amenity to the hotel suite where I had been holed up for the past three days.

I pulled a Coors Light out of the fridge. I heard the excited voice of anchorman Wes Howser, Channel 7, The News Voice of Tidewater. I walked back, sat down on the foot of the bed, twisted the top off the beer, and tossed it in the corner with the others. As I listened, I took out my knife and cut a generous slice of lime, squeezed it into my beer. A Coorsona.

Wes Howser was sitting behind his news desk. The words "Breaking News" flashed across the bottom of the screen as he spoke, "We hate to interrupt your normally scheduled programming, but we have just learned the grand jury, hearing evidence in the Terrance Lundsford murder case, has concluded. Chief Petty Officer Nigel Logan, the prime suspect, is believed to be guilty of the violent, execution-style murder of local rapper Terrance "T-Daddy" Lundsford. Sherry Stone is outside the Virginia Beach Courthouse, waiting for the official word. Let's go to Sherry now."

The screen switched to a head shot of an attractive blond. She stood on the steps of the courthouse and she wasn't alone. Reporters from other news stations were on location, too. They were all awaiting a press conference expected at any moment. She was attentive, listening to Wes Howser, waiting for her lead-in.

"So, Sherry, what can you share with us? What is the latest?" asked the anchorman.

Nodding her head in acknowledgment before speaking, she said, "Wes, these courthouse steps behind me will soon set the stage for what is sure to be a dramatic press conference with Virginia Beach District

Attorney, Blair Westhoven. Our sources tell us the grand jury hearing and reviewing evidence in the high-profile Lundsford case has concluded. And now we await the decision on whether the state's evidence is strong enough to indict Chief Petty Officer Nigel Logan for the murder of Terry Lundsford."

Wes Howser asked, "Is there any sign, or have you heard any word about what the decision might be?"

Before she answered, the courthouse doors flew open with DA Westhoven stepping out toward the podium. The news crews ran up the steps, cameras were flashing, and the reporters were all screaming the same question in fourteen different ways. Westhoven held out his open palms toward the eager reporters to quiet them. He wouldn't be taking questions, but making a prepared statement. He stood there trying to portray firm confidence, but I could see the truth. His eyes revealed the hidden expression of a broken man, disappointed, even embarrassed.

I took another drink of beer and reached over to grab the remote control. As DA Westhoven spoke, I hit the red button. The TV screen went dark with a crackling spark of static. The room became excessively quiet. I took another pull from my beer, set it down on the dresser, and crawled back on top of the bed. I stared at the ceiling again, deep in thought. There were so many things to think about, so many decisions to make.

I turned my head toward the lampshade, looking for my spider. It was gone, nowhere to be found. It had slipped away unnoticed. I smiled and closed my eyes.

I felt well-rested when I rose from my quick nap. It had been a long ordeal. With the grand jury news behind me, it was time to get the hell out of there. I had had enough of hotel living. I grabbed my bag, collected the few things I had brought with me and slammed the door, leaving the keycard on the dresser. There was still the better part of a twelve-pack in the fridge. I figured the cleaning staff could make good use of them.

As I stepped out into the Tidewater sun, I noticed a clean, black Crown Vic with tinted windows parked next to my truck, an older model Ford F-150. As I got closer, the driver's door on the Vic opened and Detective Larry Anderson stepped out. He closed the door and leaned against the hood; arms crossed, giving him a non-wavering defiant air. It was an attempt to intimidate. It didn't impress me.

My attorney, the local police, and the prosecution all knew I was at the hotel. Nobody else did, though. It was my Skipper's idea to get off the ship for a few days, especially while the case was being heard. He didn't want or need the distraction for the ship's company. It was already difficult enough, and he felt my presence would only make things worse. And while he never said it, I knew it was to protect me. If things hadn't worked out as they had, he wanted to spare me the embarrassment of being escorted off the ship in handcuffs.

"Where do you think you are going?" the detective asked.

"Larry, I fail to see where that remains to be any of your damn business," I replied. "But if you have to know, I am returning to my ship."

"We're not on a first-name basis, Chief."

"Where I come from, Chief is my first name, Larry."

"You're a cocky, smug bastard, aren't you?"

"Go screw yourself."

I proceeded to my truck and stopped at the door, thought for a second, then turned, "Let me ask you something. What is it you guys feel worse about? That you couldn't get an indictment on me for the killing of T-Daddy, or that you completely fucked up the arrest and prosecution of Lundsford? Huh? Come on. Have an honest moment with me here."

He stared at me, speechless. Then he found something cheap to say.

"Go to hell, Logan."

Climbing up into my truck, I said, "That's what I thought. And you have the nerve to call me a smug bastard. You're a piece of work, detective. At least I sleep at night with a clear conscience."

I started my truck and let it idle for a bit. I sat behind the wheel and rolled my window down for one last question. I already knew the answer but wanted to strike a nerve.

"So detective, when can I have my weapon back? It's mine, you know, and I want it returned."

Part of the evidence against me was the weapon used in the killing. It was mine, a 9mm Beretta. There was no denying that. They found the gun at the crime scene. Ballistics showed the single fatal bullet was fired from its chamber, and the gun's registration led the police straight to me.

"You're not getting the weapon back, asshole. It remains evidence in the case and tied up in the continuing investigation."

I smiled.

The detective continued, "You may think this is funny and that it's all over, but it's not. We're going to keep digging. I know you killed him, and I will *nail* you for it."

"I don't know detective. Sometimes... things have a funny way of working themselves out. It seems to me justice has already been served. So, go ahead, keep looking. Perhaps one day you will find your killer. If you do, if that day comes, if I were you, I'd shake his hand. See ya around, Larry."

I rolled up my window and backed out of the parking space. The detective remained leaning up against his car as I drove out of the lot, painfully slow. I wanted to burn this memory in his brain. A day and an encounter he would never forget.

I drove down the waterfront toward the pier where my ship was moored. They tied it up out on the end, behind another destroyer. I shook my head as I counted three news trucks set up outside the gate. They were damned and determined to get the follow-up story to today's news. *Not today, folks, not today.*

Amongst them was Sherry Stone of Channel 7. She had wasted no time in packing up from the courthouse and bustling here to relocate. Hard worker, dedicated, I liked that. Plus, she was more beautiful in person than on the tube. I liked that too.

I cruised by nice and slow to assess the situation, too slow, I guess. Miss Stone turned her head and our eyes met. She immediately recognized me and flashed a welcoming smile. But that was it, nothing more. She never drew attention to the fact I was there. I found that odd.

I drove on down and found a place to park. I picked up my cell phone and called the quarterdeck. Petty Office Sterling answered the phone. I recognized his voice.

"Good afternoon, USS Davenport, this is an unsecured line. How may I help you, Sir, or Ma'am?"

"Good afternoon, shipmate. This is Chief Logan. Who is on watch with you?"

"Hello, Chief. This is Petty Officer Sterling. We're all so happy with the news. Congratulations."

Sterling is a Boatswain Mate Second Class, a BM2, works in Deck Department, 1st Division. First Division is one of the toughest departments on a ship, the meat and potatoes of the Navy. The care and maintenance of the ship is their responsibility. It isn't glamorous work, but it's necessary to keep any war vessel shipshape and in fighting condition.

Sterling is exceptional and all Navy. Salt runs through his veins. I like him. He is result-driven and more squared away in his uniform than most others with much cleaner jobs. The level of responsibility and the number of people for which he is accountable exceed most of the commissioned officers on the boat. He is going to make a great chief.

"Thank you, Sterling. So, who is the OOD?" *Officer of the Day.*

"That would be Mr. Gray, Chief."

"Perfect." Mr. Gray is a Lieutenant Junior Grade from the Supply Department, a nice guy, easy to work with. "I need to come aboard, but I don't want to deal with the media at the gate. Clear it with the OOD and get the duty driver to bring the van over so I can get past these vultures. I've had enough excitement for one day."

I gave Sterling my location and sat back. My eyes were closed, head back against the headrest. I was about to doze off when a tap on the driver's side window startled me. *Man, I got to get some real rest.* I opened my eyes and saw Sterling, a big grin on his face, the right side of his lower lip slightly swollen with a dip of Copenhagen.

I rolled down my window.

Sterling said, "I figured I'd come get you myself. Jonesie, the duty driver, is covering for me on the quarterdeck."

"Good plan. Is the Skipper still on board?"

"Yes, Chief. And he knows you're about to come aboard. Mr. Gray told him. I'm also to pass the word that he would like to see you in the morning, in his stateroom, right after quarters."

"Thanks, BM2," I said. "Let's go."

Sterling never said another word on the short drive back. He was smart enough to know that if I wanted to talk, I would say something. I appreciated that. Again, he's a real pro. Had they let young Seaman Apprentice Jones come pick me up, he would have talked my ear off. He hadn't yet learned the valuable lesson that sometimes less is more.

As we approached the pier, we stopped and flashed our ID cards, protocol. No one gets in without proper credentials. As we waited for the gate to open, it didn't take the media long to figure out I was in the van. The reporters and cameramen swarmed around the van. With all the commotion and the windows rolled up, their calls were mostly unintelligible. They were all yelling their questions. All but one.

Sherry Stone was off to the side, not engaging the van. She and her crew remained away from the others and standing by the fence. She was watching from afar with the same smile as before. BM2 pulled the van onto the pier toward the ship as the guards closed the gate. I looked into the side mirror and there she was, still standing by the fence. I thought about it for a second or two, then said, "BM2. Stop the van."

I opened the door and got out. Stood by the door for a long moment, then proceeded toward her position at the fence. The other media hounds closed in around her, screaming their questions, cameras rolling. Her crew surrounded and protected her, giving her plenty of space. I got to the fence, and we exchanged glances, communicating through our eyes. She reached in her pocket and pulled out a business card, stuck it through the fence. I took it and looked it over.

Through the calls and comments of the other reporters, I heard her say, "When you're ready."

I looked up. "Thank you."

She smiled and turned toward her crew. "We're out of here, boys. No story here. Not today, anyway."

I stood at the fence and watched as she and her crew crawled back in the news van. She never looked back at me. I took that as a professional courtesy. I didn't want her to leave, but I stood there and watched as she rode away.

I turned and walked back to the van. Sterling was patient. "Are we ready, Chief?"

I flipped the card over to find another number there, handwritten. A personal cell phone, perhaps.

"Sure. Let's go."

Through the fog of my thoughts, I heard, "Well... are you, or aren't you?" The words bounced off my ears but didn't register. I heard them again, this time with the mention of my name, which prompted me to creep out of my daydream. "Dammit, Nigel. Are you, or aren't you?"

My head cleared, and I looked up. It was Red. I asked, "Huh? Are you? Are you what?"

Red said, "Brother, you are acting like one spaced-out crazy bastard. Are you all right?"

"Yeah, I'm fine. I was thinking about something. That's all."

"Anything you want to talk about?"

I thought about it for a minute, and the words of Sherry Stone came back to me again. *When you're ready.* I looked up at Red and said, "No, not today. Another day, maybe."

I shook my head to clear my noggin and put the card back in my wallet. I took a sip from my beer. It wasn't as cold as I remembered, but it helped to flush the memories.

"Now," I said. "What is it you were asking me? Am I or am I not, what?"

Red pointed at the tray of oysters and said, "Eating that last one?"

I looked down and my dozen oysters were gone, all but one. The only things that remained were some cracker crumbs and residual splashes of Crystal hot sauce in empty shells. I looked up at Red in amazement. "Really, you ate my oysters? You left me one, and now you want my permission to down it too?"

Red chuckled, "You didn't seem too interested, and they were getting cold."

"They're raw, Red! They're supposed to be cold."

Red chuckled as he said, "You're a grumpy bastard, too."

I soaked the remaining oyster with Crystal and slurped it right out of the shell. I slapped the bar to get the attention of the shuckers and threw a ten-dollar bill in the tip jar. They smiled as I twirled my finger around in the air. *Another round boys!*

THE QUESTION

T he second I stepped back aboard the ship, I knew my life there could never be the same. Memories would fade over time, but they would never erase, never disappear. The crew could never treat me as they had before. The cloud of curiosity and suspicion that had befallen me was too great. It's natural. The question would always be there, and folks would want to ask. Most would never dare.

After all the handshaking and congratulatory greetings on the quarterdeck, Petty Officer Sterling asked, "Where to, Chief? I'll usher you through the ship so nobody disturbs you."

I faced Sterling, reached out with both hands, took hold of his muscular biceps, and shook them gently. "No thanks, shipmate. I think I can manage from here. I appreciate you, though. Thanks for coming to get me."

Sterling nodded back with a grin. Then he caught me pass a subtle, non-verbal message. I took my tongue and poked out the right side of my lower lip. He smiled as he reached down and retrieved a can of Copenhagen from his left sock and handed it to me. I winked as I took a dip. I handed him the can back and slapped him on the arm. "Thanks again for everything."

"See ya in the morning, Chief."

My first line of business was to run down Marcus Towers. He's a Chief Personnelman and a workaholic. I knew he would be in his office, and that's where I found him. He was still in his khaki uniform sitting behind his desk, a fresh cup of hot steaming coffee in front of him. He looked up and stood as I came through the door.

"Nigel! Good to see you, buddy. Welcome back. Can I get you a cup of coffee?" He started toward the coffeemaker before I had a chance to decline. I love coffee, but I can't drink it that late in the day. I'd be up pacing the floor at three in the morning.

"No. No, Marcus. Thanks, but I can't drink the stuff like you."

I don't know how anyone can drink coffee like Marcus. He has a cup with him from the time he gets up through taps, always drinking. It's like his nervous system is numb to the effects of caffeine. The son of a bitch has no problem sleeping, and he's difficult to wake up in the morning. All of which is remedied by a fresh cup of steaming black Joe, to restart the vicious cycle.

He's not alone. The Navy is full of squids like him. Every ship has more than a handful of these coffee addicts. The Command Master Chief from my first ship was like that, drank coffee from dawn till dusk. In my young career, I admired and looked up to his crusty, salty ways, and I tried to emulate his coffee routine. After about three weeks, when I finally went to sleep, I realized it probably wasn't in my best interest. Nowadays, I try not to touch the stuff after 1000.

Since Marcus was already up, I allowed him to get me a bottle of water from the fridge. He handed me a Dasani and sat back down. I grabbed a chair and pulled it up to his desk. He made small talk about the ship and crew to make me feel comfortable, like things were perfectly normal. But they weren't. Our minds were on other things, probably the same thing... or damn near. The conversation faded to an awkward silence, and I broke it by saying, "Marcus, there is something I need for you to do for me. And not just do, but make it a priority plus keep it under wraps. That means I need for you to handle everything, not get your personnel involved at all."

Marcus put his coffee cup down and leaned forward on his desk as I explained my desire to retire quietly and as soon as possible. He gave a halfhearted attempt to talk me out of it, but knew he was wasting his time. He saw it in my eyes. Plus, I think he understood the practicality of the decision.

We talked about the details, a possible effective date, and what could be expected. I stood up, shook his hand, and told him I would have my official written request to him in the morning. He remained seated and returned a smile of acknowledgment, disappointment on his face. Then he asked, "So I guess this means no retirement ceremony, huh?"

I smiled back and said, "No. No ceremony. But don't worry; I'll plan something with the mess, but until then, not a word. Okay?"

Marcus nodded again, and I headed out of his spaces. Stepping through the door, he stopped me and said, "Nigel. Can I ask you something? Just between me and you."

"What is it Marcus?"

I knew the question. I saw it written on his face. It was the one question everybody wanted to ask. He could tell by the look on my face I knew what he wanted to know. It created an uncomfortable moment for him. He shook his head and said, "Nothing, Nigel. I'm sorry. It's nothing. No big deal."

I nodded my head with a smile and stepped out into the passageway.

Officer's Call and morning muster is a daily ritual. The entire crew gathers on the flight deck to get their morning marching orders and to review the POD, the *Plan of the Day*. There was nothing of great significance published, but that didn't mean my guys wouldn't have plenty to do. The U.S. Coast Guard had just published the latest Notice to Mariners, and there were plenty of changes that would require the charts to be updated. A tedious but necessary task for safe, effective navigation. Even in port, a quartermaster's job is never done.

I knew Skip's routine like clockwork. He would have breakfast in his stateroom at 0800. It would be a light morning meal: black coffee, an English muffin with peanut butter, and some flavor of Greek yogurt, maybe some fresh fruit. I could have knocked and entered. I have an open-door policy with Skip, but I decided I would give him plenty of time to enjoy his chow.

At 0830, I banged on the door with my signature knock, two quick knuckle raps, a pause, and a final single rap. From the other side of the door, I heard, "Chief! Come on in."

The shipboard living quarters of a commanding officer are quite cozy and roomy compared to the rest of the crew. A well-deserved perk from years of dedication and service. The Skipper's quarters were like a small one-room efficiency apartment, not huge, but spacious enough to serve as the perfect retreat from the daily stresses associated with the care and maintenance of a naval vessel and the 427 souls that worked her.

He sat at his dining room table, finishing his breakfast. As I stepped through the door, I saw him waving me in. His steward was picking up dirty dishes from the table. "Come in. Please come in. Have a seat. Coffee?"

"That would be nice, thanks."

"Petty Officer Bailes, bring Chief Logan a cup of coffee. Make it one of the big mugs, heavy cream, and no sugar."

The coffee was exceptional, not the normal kettle-brewed stuff found on the mess decks, or the chief's mess. It was fresh ground and aromatic. For Skip, even the best is barely good enough. But again, he deserves it.

"You sent word, Captain. You wanted to see me?"

He was nodding his head as he sipped his coffee. "Yes, Chief, but wait."

The steward, Bailes, was hanging around doing some tidying up, or at least that was the appearance he was trying to give. I knew better. He was hanging around with attentive ears. There wasn't anyone that wouldn't have wanted to be a fly on the wall during my visit with Skip. And if Petty Officer Bailes could collect some detail of interest for the rest of the crew, he would be a rumor-mill hero.

"That is all Bailes. Please come back and finish your cleaning later. Leave me with Chief Logan so we can chat in private, if you please."

"Aye, Aye, sir." And Bailes left the space. We watched as he departed.

Skip turned to me and said, "Good kid. Damn good cook. But he's as damn nosy as they come."

"Aren't they all?" I said.

He said nothing for a while and finally asked, "How are you, Nigel?"

"I'm doing okay, Skipper. As good as anyone that just escaped a murder indictment. I guess."

"Drop the formalities. No more Skipper shit, got it?"

"Sure, Charlie. Thanks."

Captain Charlie Matthews is my commanding officer. I have had the honor and privilege of serving with him on several occasions. By sheer luck, or by divine intervention, we've spent a good part of both of our careers together under three different commands, so we've both watched each other grow and blossom. When he made lieutenant commander, we celebrated over a bottle of single malt scotch and waited for the sun to show itself across an Italian horizon. When I made Chief, it was he that pinned on my anchors.

We were more than friends; we were family. I was at the hospital during the birth of two of his three children. He and his sweet wife Caroline have two sons, Max and Andy, and the eldest, a beautiful daughter, Grace.

"Charlie. I'm so sorry if this entire ordeal has brought you and Caroline renewed pain and sorrow. I'm sure it has had to unwind some of the healing that time brings."

Charlie looked at his coffee cup. Said nothing.

"Charlie. How is Grace?"

Charlie looked up, eyes slightly misted over, took a sip of coffee, and said, "She's doing alright it seems, except for the nightmares. They've returned. She is back in counseling. That was her idea. She is so damn mature for a twenty-year-old."

I said nothing, letting him talk.

"I spoke with her last night. After hearing the news, she called to talk about you, Nigel. She's more worried about you than about herself. Damn kid is amazing. Keeping her grades up, too. We're so proud of her."

"We all are," I said. "Like you said, she's amazing. A hell of a lot stronger than you or me."

It had been almost nineteen months since Grace and a girlfriend were driving home from a party. Grace consumed too much alcohol and passed out in the back seat. Casey, the girlfriend, took what she thought was a shortcut. She was wrong and found herself lost in an unfamiliar, undesirable part of Norfolk. A bad part of town.

Totally confused, Casey stopped and put the car in park at an intersection to get her bearings. She had her face in her smartphone pulling up a map when the driver's side door flung open. Casey was pulled from the car and slung into the street. It was a carjacking, and while Casey lay in the street, she watched in horror as her car raced away. It took a right turn at the next intersection and disappeared. The car was gone, so was Grace.

They found the car the next morning on a road outside of town. Grace was still in the car, badly beaten and raped. It was a parent's greatest nightmare come true. Charlie and his wife Caroline were devastated, and their hearts torn as they watched their little girl cope with the difficulties such horror brings.

The difficulties didn't stop there. Justice served can make things better, but it will never reverse the clock and put things back to how it used to be. It's not like a stolen car, where they catch the thief, send them off to jail, and they return the car undamaged. No. What happened to Grace is permanent, and what they took away from her can never be replaced. But when no justice is served, that is the greatest insult.

Casey was sure it was the local rapper, T-Daddy Lundsford, that had pulled her from the car and drove away. She had never seen T-Daddy in person, but she had seen many of his promotional posters for local shows he had done. Plus, Terrance "T-Daddy" Lundsford was no stranger to trouble. It was common knowledge that "T-Daddy" was your typical gangster thug and regular person of interest in several past crimes. He had a reputation and made the news often.

As it came time to testify in the carjacking charge, Casey got scared. Her level of certainty that sent police immediately to Lundsford's home waned. Charlie and I sat in the courtroom and felt our veins turn to ice as we heard her say, "I think it was him. It sort of looked like him. To be honest, I can't be totally sure." At that point, the case was blown. Even though they pulled his fingerprints from inside in the car, her testimony was enough to hang the jury. They escorted him back to his cell where he awaited trial for the crimes against Grace Matthews.

One week later, I was on my sailboat, *MisChief*, relaxing after a long, exhausting day. When my cell phone rang, I was enjoying a second pour of neat bourbon. I looked at my phone. Charlie Matthews lit up the middle of the screen. I pressed talk. "Yes, sir. Chief Logan here."

"Nigel. It's Charlie." I could sense an urgency in his voice. The line went quiet for a moment, then he said, "They are going to let the bastard go. The piece of shit is going to walk."

"Release him? Release who, Charlie?"

Then I heard the name Lundsford and went numb. Charlie continued talking, trying to explain what had happened, but I couldn't hear him. I had tuned everything out with my own dazed sickness. I came back to the conversation when I heard Charlie call my name. "Nigel. Nigel, are you there?"

"Yes. Yes, I'm here. I'm sorry. This is awful news. Now please, I'm sorry. Tell me again what this is all about?"

Turns out Lundsford's defense attorney, James Milford, was reviewing the case against his client when he noticed a serious flaw with the handling of the prosecution's cornerstone evidence. The DNA collected from Grace, Lundsford's DNA. They mishandled it. They could not properly account for the chain of custody from the time they captured his specimen to the time of its receipt at the lab. A huge mistake.

Milford and the prosecution team met with the judge to review and argue for and against the evidence's admissibility in court. Milford prevailed, and the judge threw the evidence out. The case became unhinged. Grace could not clearly identify her attacker, and the prosecution's entire case hinged on the DNA connecting him with the victim.

The findings sickened the district attorney, but he wasn't willing to go to court with only paper-thin evidence. The DA wasn't willing to risk a not-guilty verdict that would prevent them from ever going after Lundsford at some later time. Plus, to lose such a case wouldn't look good on his resume. They dropped the charges.

I listened to the pain and anger in Charlie's voice. I was angry too, mad as hell. *How could they have screwed this up? How?* What little satisfaction a guilty verdict could have brought to Grace and her family was suddenly gone. It vanished. And the likelihood police would unveil additional evidence suitable enough to bring another arrest and the case back to court was questionable. And worst of all, he would be back on the streets, free to do this again and probably would.

I paced the salon of my boat, back and forth, back and forth, listening. It was the best I could do under the circumstances. Sometimes the best part of a genuine friend is their ears; I gave him mine for as long as he needed them. I finally asked if he wanted me to come over. He told me no, that he and Caroline needed some time. And the line went quiet.

I stopped pacing in front of my navigation station and reached down and opened the bottom drawer and said, "Love you, brother. You know that, right? If you or Caroline need anything, I'm a phone call away. Don't hesitate to call."

Charlie said, "I know Nigel. It's just that we've all been through so much, not to mention Grace. Now to have this happen. What in the world are we going to do?"

Anger seeped from my pores as cold sweat. I stood looking down into the drawer, reached down, and said, "You're not going to do anything but take care of Grace, your family, and yourself. Do you hear me?"

Charlie said nothing. All I heard was breathing.

Inside the drawer, I gently folded back the black oiled cloth that covered my 9mm Beretta. I picked it up. The blue steel was icy to my skin, but the pistol grip felt good in the palm of my hand, comfortable. It was like wearing a favorite hat that knows every contour of your head, fitting perfectly. I stood staring at it and finally said, "Charlie, I know it doesn't seem like it now, but everything is going to be alright. I promise. Kiss Caroline and Grace for me and try to get some rest."

I took a long draw of coffee and realized I was hungrier than I thought. I looked back toward the door to Charlie's galley and asked, "Can I grab an English muffin or something?"

"Don't be ridiculous. You can have whatever you want. Let me get Petty Officer Bailes back in here and I'll have him heat one up for you."

"That's okay. I think I can manage." I got up, went into the galley, found the English muffins, halved one, and put it in the toaster. "Can I get you anything while I'm up?"

He declined. Then I said, "Charlie, you know it's time for me to leave, right? My time's up. I can't stay any longer."

I walked back to the table when Charlie said, "What are you talking about? You just got here a few minutes ago."

I sat back down and said, "Not leave, as in, leave here now. Leave for good, that's what I mean. I can't stay in this town right now. I've got to go."

Charlie asked, "You are putting in for a transfer?"

I reached into my back pocket and handed him a copy of the paperwork I had already given to Marcus. He unfolded it and studied its contents. A look of shock and concern flew across his face, and then he collected himself and returned to his normal professional deportment. He folded it back up and handed it back to me. "Is this what you want, to retire?"

"Hell no. It's not what I want, but I don't feel like I have any other choice. It doesn't matter where I go in the Navy, this Lundsford thing will always loom over my head and career. I think it is best for all concerned."

"Where will you go?"

"I'm not sure. Away from Norfolk. That's for damn sure."

The room got quiet, and we left each other to our thoughts. He finished his coffee while I polished off mine and the English muffin. We said little. I stood up and walked around to Charlie's side of the table and patted my dear friend on the back, a parting gesture. And, at that moment, we both transitioned back to our normal naval presence, commanding officer and chief petty officer.

"If that will be all, sir, I should check on the guys in my division."

"That will be all, Chief."

"Thank you, sir."

I headed back to the door, and before I could get there, the captain got my attention. "Chief?"

I slowly turned, but said nothing. I looked at the skipper and, much like with Chief Towers, I could see the question brewing in his eyes. It was there, plain as day. The captain didn't say a word, so I said, "Captain, sir. There is one thing that will never change in this Navy of ours. And it's that a ship's captain doesn't always need to know how his chiefs get things accomplished. How things get done. They accept it. Some questions are better left unasked. It's the way it's always been, and it's the way it will always be."

He closed his eyes and returned a slow nod. When he opened his eyes, I was gone.

The End

THANK YOU!

If you enjoyed *Finding Port St. Joe*, there are a few things you could do to make this author incredibly happy.

First, provide a short, honest review at Amazon. Those reviews mean so much more than you could imagine. It doesn't have to be long. We appreciate *star only* reviews too.

Second, if you like Nigel Logan and the gang, please consider signing up for my monthly newsletter. There, you will gain some insight into Nigel Logan and the knucklehead that created him. Oh... That would be me. PLUS! You can grab a **FREE** copy of *The Cuban,* a Nigel Logan novella I wrote just for you. And... If you join us, I will make you this one promise: *I will not fill your inbox with junk and SPAM.* Sign up at www.KirkJockell.com

And the third thing is, contact me. I love to hear from readers. Let me know what you thought of the book. It would make my day more than you can imagine.

Email: Kirk@KirkJockell.com
Facebook: www.facebook.com/KirkJockellAuthor
Website: www.KirkJockell.com
Book Bub: www.BookBub.com/Kirk S Jockell

ACKNOWLEDGMENTS

My most sincere appreciation goes out to so many people. None more so than my wonderful wife, Joy. She is my bride, my partner, my rock, and number one supporter. To do things without her would be impossible. Her love and encouragement are nothing short of amazing.

During my journey as a writer, my friends (old and new) mean so much to me. They provide the greatest support imaginable. There are too many to mention, but you know who you are. Thanks so much! You help to keep the engine running.

Getting emails from readers is one of the best parts of this job. Thanks to all of you that have done so. They are more valuable than the royalties. Words cannot express the appreciation I have for each of you. Thanks to you all!

Then, there are those *real folks* that take the greatest risk of all and make cameo appearances in these books. Folks like my buddies Brian Bowen. Thanks for playing along. Then there is, of course, WOYS Oyster Radio 106.5 on your FM dial (previously 100.5). I can't imagine the Forgotten Coast without Oyster Radio.

Then, there are the folks that keep me from looking too stupid, which isn't easy. That I can promise. The editing and proofing team: Jan Lee and Tim "Coach" Slauter. Thanks, guys. We did it again.

ABOUT THE AUTHOR

Kirk Jockell is an American writer and the creator of The Nigel Logan Action Series. Port St. Joe, Florida is home, but he sleeps most nights in Flowery Branch, Georgia, where his wife continues to work one of those regular day jobs she loves (Yuck). He patiently awaits the day she can join him in retirement and trade it all in for a simpler life back down on The Forgotten Coast. Kirk is a sailor and an avid photographer of sailboats. He loves to fish, throw his cast net for mullet, listen to music (Pop Country doesn't count), play his guitar, and drive his Bronco on the beach. Kirk lives with his lovely wife Joy, a rescued bluetick coonhound named Nate (#98Nate), and a tuxedo cat named Mr. Hemingway.

OTHER WORKS BY KIRK S. JOCKELL

The Tales from Stool 17 Series
Finding Port St. Joe (Book 1)
Trouble in Tate's Hell (Book 2)
Dark Days of Judgment (Book 3)

More Nigel Logan Books
Tough Enough (Prequel)
Tupelo Honey (Book 4)
Traffic (Book 5)
Tidewater Moon (Book 6)
Tormented (Book 7)
Trapped (Book 8)
The Cuban (Novella)

Standalone Books
Michael